ARTS AND GRAFT

Sally Reid

Also by Sally Reid:

The Freedom Fence

Copyright © 2013 Sally Reid
All rights reserved.
ISBN-13: 9781499525519
ISBN-10: 1499525516

Library of Congress Control Number: 2014908987
CreateSpace Independent Publishing Platform
North Charleston, South Carolina

PROLOGUE

"I think you two should take it outside. You've both had too much to drink and I don't want any trouble in here," said Teddy Kerrigan, owner and operator of Kerrigan's, a popular pub in Graent, Ireland, just outside of Dublin.

"Fine," he said. "I don't want any trouble either." He turned to the girl next to him and asked, "Are you coming with me or are you staying with this drunk?"

"I'm staying with Tommy," she said. "He needs my help."

"Well, if that's your decision. But I'm warning you; he's no good for you. I love you and I hate to see you settle for the likes of him."

Tommy lunged for him at that point and nearly fell to the floor. "Sure," he said to her as he looked at Tommy weaving unsteadily on his feet. "Good choice." He left the pub and as he headed for his car he could hear her arguing with Tommy about driving home drunk. He thought about the time before Tommy had moved to town and how close he had been to her. He had believed with all his heart that they would marry someday. He would take over his father's business and they would raise a family of dark-haired, blue-eyed children. That had all changed when Tommy started making advances toward her. She had resisted at first, but eventually she had fallen for his lines. Everyone else knew Tommy would never settle down with one woman. He had already cheated on her with several others; he had even left town with one of them and was gone for a week, but she always took him back, each time forgiving him for cheating on her.

He stepped into the shadow of the cluttered alley as she and Tommy exited the pub. She was saying that she would walk home rather than ride in a car with someone as drunk as Tommy was. She tried to take the keys to his car from his hand, but he was an obstinate drunk and he yelled at her to walk home if she wanted, but nobody was going to take his keys. He was a man, and no woman was going to tell him what to do.

He watched as she quickly caught a cab to her apartment on the other side of town. He didn't worry about her safety. The real danger had been in her possibly getting into the car with a drunk driver. What he did worry about was whether Tommy would kill himself in the car. He could live with that, but he couldn't live with the possibility that Tommy might kill someone else in the process. He stepped forward willing to talk Tommy into a truce and a ride home rather than let him drive in that condition. But something happened. Tommy became mean and then violent. Tommy threw his keys to the ground and swung both fists wildly in his direction. He felt he had no choice but to defend himself. He swung once and made contact with Tommy's jaw and down he went.

"Get up Tommy. I'll give you a ride home. We can settle this business about you and her at a time when we're both sober." Tommy didn't move. He shoved the body with his boot and still there was no response. He moved toward Tommy's head and saw blood seeping into the packed dirt. He looked closer and saw that Tommy had landed on a length of angle iron and that it had penetrated his skull between his eyes. In the seconds since he had fallen, Tommy's blood had started to pool underneath him. He knew what he should do. He should run to the pub and tell Teddy to call an ambulance. He also knew that if he did that, that he would be suspected of intentionally killing Tommy after the fight they had just had in the pub. And even if he weren't accused of murder, she would never forgive him and she would be lost to him forever. There was obviously nothing that could be done to save Tommy. A person can't have a thick hard piece of iron penetrate his skull and survive.

There seemed to be only one thing that he could do. He found Tommy's keys on the ground, walked to the parking lot, got his car, and brought it around to the alley. He tried to pick Tommy up and intended to place him in the car. But when he put his arms under Tommy's shoulders and lifted, he realized that the iron was stuck in his skull and he was going to have to pull it out. So he did. But he was not a cruel and heartless person. The act of pulling that iron out of the skull of a person who had been living and breathing minutes before was abhorrent to him, but he felt he had no choice. He pulled on Tommy's red hair until his face came free, and then with a strength that only comes from fear, he managed to get the upper half of Tommy's torso lying across the back of the car's boot, and then he lost it. He threw up all the food and beer he had recently consumed. He threw up on Tommy, he threw up on the angle iron, and he threw up on the already blood-drenched earth. When he recovered himself, he lifted Tommy by the legs and stuffed him inside the car, closing the lid on the body.

He looked at the spot where Tommy had lain. The blood was all but covered with vomit, something that was not unusual and would hardly be noticed in this alley late in the evening. A few kicks of dirt in the direction of the evidence covered it completely. The rain that was forecast for the early morning would take care of it. If someone were looking for blood they might find it, but if he had any luck at all, it would just look as if someone had had too much to drink. But now what to do with the car? He knew that a home in town was empty temporarily because old man Kindrick was in the hospital recovering from gall bladder surgery. If he could get the car around Kindrick's garage and into the shed in the far corner of the yard, it would give him some time to think about his next move. He got in the car and moved the driver's seat back to accommodate his six foot frame and drove the few blocks to the house. Kindrick lived in a neighborhood of grand old homes with expansive back yards. In addition, each yard was encircled with hedges and trees designed to ensure privacy. That made it perfect for his purposes.

He pulled onto Liffey Street and drove the length of it to make sure that no houses were still lit. When he was certain that all the neighbors had turned in for the night he pulled into the Kindrick driveway with the lights off, aimed toward to the right of the garage, and drove around the perimeter toward the shed in the back. He had to get out and open the shed doors and move some bags of mulch and planting soil out of the way, but he was careful to do so without making any noise. He drove into the shed and closed the doors. He thought about going back to the pub and getting his own car before he went home, but he was afraid that anyone who had left the pub in the time it took him to dispose of Tommy's body would wonder why it had still been there at closing time but was gone later in the night. That sort of thing might be important if Tommy's body were discovered. He felt he might be better off leaving it there and saying that as soon as he left the pub, he walked home to avoid driving while intoxicated. He would get it in the morning. He headed toward his rooms over his father's garage making sure that he wasn't seen. He ducked into the darkness or the cover of trees whenever he saw a car approaching. He felt he had made it without being detected.

When he got home finally, he stepped into the shower to wash away the blood, the dirt, the vomit, after which he wrapped the clothes he had been wearing in newspaper and placed them in a garbage bag to be disposed of in the morning. He would eventually have to decide what to do with Tommy's car and his body, but for now he felt he had a bit of time to do that. He breathed a sigh of relief as he heard the rain coming down hard and he thought of all the evidence of what had happened being washed away.

1

Anna Kelly stood next to her friend Sarah Ryan as they watched Braden Ahern's coffin being lowered into the ground. Sarah and Anna were the very best of friends even though they had known each other for only a year. They were alike in temperament, but different in many other ways. Sarah's hair was dirty blonde and she stood about five feet four inches tall. Anna had thick raven-colored hair and deep blue eyes and was about three inches taller. Sarah's figure was fit and athletic while Anna was svelte and graceful. Sarah lived on an estate that would have suited the royal family, while Anna's home, though still lovely, was much smaller and more understated. Sarah had a fleet of cars from which to choose on any given day, while Anna drove her one Mercedes convertible exclusively. When the two rode together Sarah could choose from a string of horses, while Anna had the one horse that she had loved and ridden for several years. Sarah was an American who dressed for comfort. For example, today she wore a simple black dress with black flat shoes suitable for walking on a cemetery lawn, while Anna wore a designer suit, carried a designer bag, and wore designer shoes, platforms to accommodate the sod, but still no flats for her. If the shoes were not comfortable, so be it. She would remove them later when there was no one to see. There were more differences between them, but they loved and admired each other in spite of them.

As they stood side by side, a study in contrast, they both thought of the adventure Sarah and Braden Ahern had had, and remembered him with great fondness. Braden was a retired teacher who had touched the lives of half of the people in Dublin and half of them were there to pay their final respects. Mr. Ahern was more than a teacher to many of them; he was a mentor, a confidant, and a role model. He was known for his love of literature and fine clothes. He would be sorely missed. He and Sarah had become close since her arrival in Ireland and she had been instrumental in arranging his funeral. In fact they had spent hours in recent months discussing just how he would make his exit after he finally confided in her that he was going to die soon. The final portion of the funeral service was to be a chorus of all the attendees singing his favorite song, *When Irish Eyes Are Smiling*, as they made their way from the grave site. It was begun by a dear friend and fellow teacher of Mr. Ahern's, and picked up by several in the crowd who were aware of his wishes, so that eventually almost everyone in attendance was singing along. He would have liked that. Anna leaned over and whispered into Sarah's ear, "Braden's eyes are smiling down right now."

After the service Sarah was going to St. Gerald's, the retirement home where Braden Ahern spent his last days. There was a celebration of his life planned that involved his favorite foods, his favorite music, and readings of his favorite poetry. Anna would not be attending because of a prearranged meeting, so as they reached their respective cars, Sarah and Anna waved their good byes, and still singing, got in and drove away from the cemetery.

2

Anna drove the short distance from the cemetery to her home. She approached the gates to Kellenwood with the same feelings she had every time she returned home. She loved her house, not just because it was beautiful, but because of what it represented to her and to her husband, Carl.

Carl and Anna had both grown up in Graent, but they had not known one another except by sight. So when they met on campus at Dublin Business School, they would say hello and keep walking. But after the same thing occurred several times in the first week of classes, they felt destined to get to know one another. It started off with a Guinness at a nearby pub and ended with a happy marriage that had lasted ten years so far with no sign of a waning of affections between them. Carl had majored in business and had a prestigious job offer before he graduated. He was at the top of his class in school and the top of his accounting firm within two years. It was a meteoric rise that was well deserved.

Anna had majored in journalism and after graduation had spent the first summer planning a simple but memorable wedding. They had little money and were aware enough of the ways of the world of finance to spend only what they could afford on the wedding and reception. No two carat diamond ring for her, no fancy reception with a grand, expensive cake, and certainly no designer gown. She wore sandals and a simple white cotton dress intended more for the beach than for a wedding, yet

Anna made it look beautiful. She carried a bouquet of white daisies and wore a wreath of matching flowers on her head. Carl wore a dark gray suit and a huge smile. Her mother took decorating lessons for a month so she could make precisely the cake that Anna wanted. It was a beautiful day and a beautiful wedding.

Soon after they were married Anna was hired as an arts columnist at the *Graent Gazette*. She loved her job and was good at it. She had always loved art in all its forms, and though she had no skill of her own she was able to recognize it in others. Graent ten years ago was a small town with a church and cemetery, a general store, a food market and petrol station combined, and four pubs. It had been that way for as long as Anna could remember, but it began to change when people from Dublin and other large cities wanted a quiet place to spend their weekends. They bought property from locals for more than the property was worth and either renovated homes or tore them down and started over. There were pluses and minuses to this influx of out-of-towners, but one of the things that happened was that a class of people who loved and bought art at inflated prices moved into the area and Graent began to develop a reputation as a mecca for artists and art lovers. This made Anna's work easy. There was always something to write about and always a showing or sale of some sort on the weekends. She started to write articles for national magazines to supplement her newspaper income and she became as busy as Carl. Eventually, between them their income soared to far more than they ever had imagined it could as young kids growing up in a tiny Irish village.

When Carl suggested that they should move from their four room apartment into an actual house, Anna was afraid. She came from a family that lived from paycheck to paycheck with never any extra for the things young girls enjoyed, and she did not want to live the rest of her life that way. But Carl persisted. He reminded her that he was the business major and that in the market of the time they could afford a much grander house than they would normally, because the prices of larger luxury homes had dropped drastically. He said it would be a good investment and that they should be putting their money into a home instead of rent. So they started house hunting and when they found the home they would later name Kellenwood she fell in love for the second time in her life.

The house was set on a knoll, drawing the eye up toward the sky. It was constructed of white stone with black shutters and doors, and black trim. It was symmetrical with a three story center portion large enough for a home of generous proportion. But added to each side was a two story addition built at a slight angle to the center. The double center doors opened into a spacious foyer that was full of light and dignity. It was walk in ready; the furniture and draperies would stay. Though Anna had a great eye for decorating and definite ideas of her own, she looked at the house as already perfect and didn't want to change a thing. The sale moved quickly and she and Carl moved in and felt at home at once. It was as if the home had been built with them in mind.

So on this day she drove up to the front door and smiled in satisfaction. Her life was perfect, almost. But she tried not to think about the imperfection, the heartache. She entered her home and took the winding stairway to her rooms on the second floor. She removed the designer suit and shoes and replaced them with designer jeans and high-heeled designer sandals and a designer short-waist jacket over a designer tee shirt. She replaced the black purse she had carried to the funeral with a large brown hobo bag and headed back to her car for the short trip to her meeting. She and Carl were to meet a contractor who was going to help with a pet project of Anna's. Since Anna had left her job the year before she had started one project after the other and left many of them unfinished, but her heart was in this one and she was not going to allow this idea to fade.

3

As Anna pulled up in front of Kelly's Pub to wait for Carl to arrive her phone rang. It was Carl calling to say he would be unable to meet with her after all. "We have a real emergency here and I just can't leave the office right now. I'm sorry; I know you wanted me to take the meeting with you, but the thing is, I truly believe that you have this project well in hand and I would just muddy the waters."

"If you absolutely can't be here there's no point in trying to convince you, but I do wish you could."

"I know, but this is your inheritance, your house, your baby."

Anna winced at the use of that particular turn of phrase, but said nothing.

"You have my complete faith," said Carl, "and you can bring me up to speed tonight. I might be a bit late, but wait up for me and tell me all about it."

"Okay, I will. I'm already here at the pub so I'll go in now and let you get back to your emergency. Good luck with that, whatever it is."

"Thanks, I may need it. See you later."

"Bye Love."

"Crap," she said to herself as she got out of the car and walked toward the pub. "Two things I don't like are walking into a pub alone and meeting with contractors without Carl." It wasn't that she didn't feel that she, a woman, could deal with workmen, but she felt that Carl was just better at thinking of the right things to ask. But it was what it was and so she took a deep breath and opened the door. She entered the pub and looked for someone that she didn't know by sight hoping that there wouldn't be a lot of choices for her. She spotted an incredibly handsome, well-dressed man in his thirties with dark slightly-graying hair and beautiful green eyes sitting alone at a table with a pint in front of him. He was reading a set of important looking papers. There was another lone ale drinker in a plaid flannel shirt and with holes in his jeans. She approached him, but was stopped when she heard someone call her name. It was the other gentleman who was obviously aware of her presumption. He smiled a knowing smile and asked if she were looking for him. Anna felt as if she had been caught in the act of profiling.

"Are you Shane Anderson?" she asked.

"I am." He nodded in the direction of the plaid shirted man and said, "I'm sorry if you are disappointed."

"I'm the one who should be sorry. I think I'll just leave and come back in again if you don't mind."

"That's not necessary. Will you join me for a pint?"

"Sure, I'd love one. I'm Anna Kelly." She extended her hand and they shook.

He asked the bar tender for another like his and got up and pulled out the chair for Anna. "I was interested in what you had to say about this project when we spoke on the phone. If you don't mind my curiosity, I'd like a little background on it. It helps me to have a story to work with."

"That's an interesting approach for a contractor to take."

"I see myself as a story teller. I look at a building and ask it what it wants to say. In this case you can help tell the tale."

The pint of ale was delivered to the table and Anna began to tell him what she had in mind. "Alright. Well, the house belonged to my grandparents. My grandmother died years ago and my parents and my grandfather didn't have much to do with one another after that. My grandmother had been the glue that held the family together and I loved her dearly. My parents both died, my mother of cancer about eight years ago, and my father in a car accident a year later. I am an only child so when my grandfather died a few months ago, I inherited his home. He had lived there for a long time by himself and I don't think that he ever cleaned or repaired anything except for the roof which was all but destroyed completely by a falling tree during a storm a few years ago. He had no choice but to replace it. So it has a good roof and beyond that everything is such a mess that I haven't even had the nerve to go through it. I'm afraid there might be uninvited four-legged guests living in there. The yard is so overgrown that the neighbors have tried many times to force him to clean it up but without success. My grandfather didn't die in the house. He fell outside in the driveway and a neighbor called the ambulance for him. He died in the hospital. I haven't been back inside the house at all. And because settling his estate took some time, the place has been unoccupied for a while."

"So that's the past; what's the future of the place as you see it?"

"For several years I wrote newspaper and magazine articles about the art community here in Graent. There are great artists living here and in nearby Dublin who sell their art for huge amounts of money. I don't need to cater to them, but what I would like is to do something for those of us who enjoy the arts, but have no current skills in producing any. I want to take my grandfather's house down to the bones and build classrooms for artists in different media to teach classes, showcase student art, and create a space for conversation about painting, pottery, photography, or any other skill that people may enjoy. It doesn't appeal to me at all, but maybe the people of Graent want to learn weaving. If that's the case then I would like to provide them with the opportunity. This is not to be a high-brow gallery for art connoisseurs only. It is a large house and I think we could make spaces large enough for classes to meet comfortably there."

"Well, I took the liberty of going to the house to check it out. It was unlocked and so I went in and walked around. Is that alright with you?"

"That's fine. I have one question for you, though. Have you seen signs of any animal infestations? That might make me a bit queezy."

He smiled and said, "I noticed evidence of mice perhaps, but there were no larger critters to be seen or evidence that there had been any. I'd say it was that roof that keeps them out. Is that what you wanted to know?"

"Yes. That is what I wanted to know. So, continue. What did you find?"

"As I said, the house was unlocked. I don't know why that is because I would have thought that someone should have seen to it when your grandfather was taken away. Anyway, someone or some people have been in and taken away a lot of the furniture and even the appliances. It has been picked over and what is left is nothing of value. The exception is the attic which is sealed. I can't say what it's like up there and I wouldn't unseal it without your permission. I would say the first step would be to empty out the entire house, take everything out and sweep it clean. When that's finished we can see more clearly what we have to work with. I have some photos of the place if you'd like to look at them." He spread the photos out on the table. There were shots of the exterior with the falling fence, the overgrown lawn and the trees with branches reaching to the ground. There were also interior shots showing the debris littering the floor.

As Anna was looking over the photos one by one, the man in the flannel shirt stood from his table and walked by on his way out the door. When he saw the photos he stopped and said, "That's the Kindrick house."

"Yes, it is," said Shane. "Do you know the place?"

"I did some yard work around there for my father's landscaping company. Then later we took out a tree that had fallen on the roof. What's going on with the place?"

"We're going to revitalize the property."

He seemed surprised at this and asked, "Can you use some help? I can do the work on the yard. We could pull up the overgrown plants and replace them, restore the planting beds, cut down the trees, that sort of thing."

"You can leave me your number if you like. We'll certainly be needing someone to clean up the yard. If we need you I'll call you."

"Here's my card. I have a bit of a landscaping business of my own. The card has all my contact information on it. Thanks for the opportunity."

"Sure. Jack Corrigan, is it?"

"Yes. I can start right away if you like. I can really use the work."

"I'll be in touch," Shane said as Jack Corrigan walked out of the pub, nervously fiddling with his cap. When he got outside the pub he leaned against the wall trying to think if working on this project might keep his world from falling apart. Everything would be fine if only he could get this job.

"So," said Anna, "When can you start?"

"Don't you want to talk about renovation costs, my fees, contracts, etc.?"

"You're right. This is why I wanted my husband here for this meeting. He would never have rushed in that way. Tell me about all those costs."

"Actually, I have worked up everything I could think of that we would need for this project and written an estimate for you. This is not a quote; there are too many variables in a project like this, so I have assessed the situation and given my best idea of what the cost will be. Any changes would be discussed with you beforehand. It's all there divided into categories so you can decide whether or not you want to use my services. I would really enjoy working on this project. Call me when you've had a chance to go over the figures. I'd like to know one way or the other."

"I will. And thank you for all the prep work. If we decide we want to go forward with this, when could you start work?"

"I have another week or so of work on a current job and can start after that. The project I had lined up after this one was canceled by divorce. I guess they don't want to fix up their house until they decide who is going to get it in the settlement."

"Bad news for them; good news for me. I'll be in touch in a couple of days."

They said their good byes and Anna left for home. On the way she drove by her grandfather's house and felt a sense of guilt and loss. The place didn't look at all the way she remembered it. That home was well maintained and smelled of baking bread and chocolate biscuits. She put her car into gear. She couldn't change the past, but she could see to it that the home her grandmother loved would see better days. And for some reason she felt that Shane Anderson was just the person to help her do it.

4

Anna waited as long as she could for Carl to come home that night, but she fell asleep with a well-worn copy of *Crime and Punishment* lying across her chest. When she woke in the morning the book was on her bed-side table with a Post-it note attached to it. "I'm sorry I missed you last night and again this morning. I'm hoping to get home for dinner at seven. I'll call you later. Love you, Carl"

Anna thought about the day ahead. She had hoped to be able to talk to Carl about the cost projections for her grandfather's house, but that wasn't going to happen. She thought of calling Sarah to go over the papers with her, but with no offense to Sarah, she hadn't lived in Ireland long enough to be familiar with local trends in construction and renovation. The person she thought of next was Fiona. She and her husband Charles had purchased an older home a few years ago and had converted it into a showplace. Surely she had learned some things during that process that could be useful to Anna. She reached for her phone and dialed Fiona's number.

"Good morning," said Fiona. "What makes you call so early? I would have bet that you wouldn't even be out of bed yet."

"You know me so well. Listen, I have some questions for you about contractors and renovating a house."

"No way. Don't you touch that house of yours! It is perfection and you know it."

"I'm not talking about my house. Well, technically it is my house, but it isn't this house. You remember my telling you that I inherited my grandfather's house, right? Well, I have some plans for it and I wondered if you'd like to give me some advice. We could go for a horseback ride. You can ride Carl's horse if you like instead of riding all the way over here."

"Ooh, I love Carl's horse. What time did you have in mind?"

"You were right when you said that I probably wasn't out of bed yet, so give me about an hour and a half to shower and have a little breakfast. Does that work for you?"

"Yes. I'll see you then."

She got out of bed, showered, and dressed in her riding clothes and runners. Her boots were in the tack room in the stable. Breakfast was a container of Greek yogurt and a cinnamon rice cake. As she was putting her spoon in the dishwasher Fiona walked in the back door to the kitchen. "Good morning. Are you ready for a ride?"

"All ready. Let's go."

Anna had called the stable ahead of time and asked Robert Callahan to saddle both horses for their ride. Robert and his wife May had come with the house. They had worked for the previous owners and were concerned that they would both be out of work. Anna and Carl had been concerned that they would have to spend an inordinate amount of time interviewing and checking the backgrounds of potential employees. Then after the hiring they would have to acquaint the new employees with a property that was new to them as well. And what about the living arrangements? The solution was simple. Anna met with the Callahans and asked if they would be willing to stay on with the same arrangements that they had had before. They agreed and they stayed on, living in the four room apartment in the west wing of the house on the top floor. They were grateful, Anna and Carl were grateful, and it had worked out for everyone.

The horses were waiting for them. Anna found her boots and put them on and the two of them mounted up. They rode to the back of Kellenwood and headed out onto government-owned lands for a ride that they knew from experience would last for about two hours.

"Okay. What's the project you're planning?"

Anna outlined the general plan for the building and told about her meeting with the contractor. "I've heard of Shane Anderson," said Fiona. "He did not do our house because he was unavailable when we started and we were too impatient to wait. He recommended the one we used and he was great. I've always heard that he's honest and reliable. He also does really good work. From everything I've heard about him from friends who've used his company, he takes pride in his results. The other thing I've heard is that when he says he's going to show up, he's there early. I don't think you can do better. What about the cost? One criticism I have heard is that he is a bit expensive. Of course, you know that you get what you pay for, and when it comes to your house you want the best."

As they rode Anna told Fiona what she could remember about the figures she had read, although she had read so many that they all seemed to blur together. "What I didn't tell him is that along with the house I inherited enough money from my grandfather's estate to refurbish that house several times over. So when it comes to decisions about materials and furnishings, I can go higher end than he has in his estimate. I can afford to spend the money to fix the house and fill it with the sorts of things the artists will need. I guess I just needed someone to tell me that I had the right man for the job."

"Who are you going to recruit for instructors?"

"I don't know. I thought once the work was underway it might be a draw for artists. Until it's ready they won't know whether they will like the place or not. I have some names from when I wrote about the art scene here in Graent, but I'm going to hold off on contacting them until there's real progress on the building."

"Good idea."

They had ridden the entire route without realizing how quickly the time had passed. When they arrived at the stable and handed over the horses, Anna returned to the tack room to change back into her runners.

As they turned toward Fiona's car she said, "If there's anything else I can do about the house just call. Otherwise, I'll see you Sunday. We meet at Sarah's this week."

"I'll see you then. Thanks again. Carl is so busy with work right now that I couldn't get his opinion, so you've been a big help."

5

Anna went into the house and talked to May about lunch. She let her know that she would be eating a light lunch and not to go to any trouble. Then she went up and took another shower, dressed in jeans and a red sweater, and walked barefoot to the desk in the study. She found the packet given to her by Shane Anderson and looked for his phone number. She dialed it and got his answering machine. She left a message for him to call her and went to the kitchen and ate her lunch while glancing through the paper.

After lunch she walked slowly upstairs, but she didn't go to her and Carl's bedroom; she went instead to the room across the hall. She opened the door slowly and stepped inside. The room was just as it had been left the day she went to the hospital.

She and Carl had taken several years to decide whether or not to have a child. They wanted to be financially able to afford one, and they wanted to have a house instead of a four room walk up. Many people raised happy kids in smaller spaces, but they had agreed early on that they wanted their children to have room to play. They needed a house and they needed a lawn. They needed a place for a swing set and a sand box. Their child would have had all of those things and more. He or she was to be an indulged child, but not a spoiled child. They would have made great parents, there was no doubt about that. But it was not to be. When Anna was seven months pregnant she had terrible cramping pains and a few long hours later there was no more baby. There would be no more baby.

As Anna settled into the rocking chair by the crib the phone rang in the other room. She quietly and slowly left the nursery and answered the phone in her room next door. It was Shane returning her call. They talked briefly about Anna's decision to hire him for the job and made arrangements to meet the next day at the house. She hung up the phone and went back to her baby's room and rocked herself to sleep. She woke to the phone ringing again, but she was unable to get to it before it stopped. May found her as she started down the stairs. It was Carl on the phone and he was not going to be home again. "If I were the jealous type I would think you had a woman somewhere."

"You know you're the only woman for me. And what are up to?"

"I just finished lunch." She chose to not tell him about her visit to the nursery. It was the one topic she didn't feel comfortable discussing with him. It was just too painful for her, and she didn't feel that it had been painful enough for him, although she was sure he suffered in his own way.

"I was wondering what you had done about the contractor."

She briefed him on the cost projections and said she felt good about the choice of Shane Anderson. She also told him that she had talked with Fiona and that she had agreed and recommended him highly. She said she had a meeting with the contractor the next day at the house on Liffey and he apologized about probably not being able to go with her. "But tomorrow's Saturday. You aren't going in to work are you?"

"I'm afraid so. When I tell you what has been going on you will understand, trust me." He suggested that she drive in to the office and share take-away dinner with him, but she declined. For her it would be a small salad, a large glass of wine, and the book she slept through last night.

"You can't work on Sunday, though. You know the rules."

"Don't worry. If this isn't resolved by Sunday I will call in sick. Deal?"

"Deal."

"It might be another late night tonight, so if I don't see you before you go to sleep, good night, Love."

There would be no work on this Sunday or any other. They rode horses with friends every Sunday. It was a ride like the ones the landed gentry used to have with the exception that there were no noisy hounds chasing after a fox. It was a group of 22 friends riding all day together after a champagne brunch at the home of one or another of the members. This Sunday was Sarah's turn to host so Anna and Carl would ride there. Other members who lived farther away would trailer their horses to and from the ride. It was wonderful fun and no one in the group would miss it without a really good reason, and an emergency at work did not qualify.

Anna hung up the phone, went to the kitchen to tell May that she would be alone for dinner and that she wanted only a salad and a glass of wine for dinner and that she was going to take a walk. She idled the rest of the day away and at dinnertime her meal was waiting for her on the sun room table. She ate lazily, since she had no schedule to keep, and when she finished her salad she put the bowl and fork in the dishwasher and carried the wine upstairs to her room. She changed from her jeans and sweater and got into bed. Her plan to read went nowhere as she fell deeply asleep and dreamed of lullabies, the smell of talcum powder, and the soft sweet baby she would hold only in her dreams.

6

Carl had already left when Anna woke in the morning. He left a note on her dresser saying that he would try to be home for dinner, but he would let her know one way or the other. She would be going to the meeting with the contractor without Carl. She spent the morning going over the photos and the plans Shane had proposed for the house in Graent and making notes of her own. She had skipped breakfast, so she had a lunch of a chicken salad sandwich and some crisps. She drank water with lunch and took another bottle for the trip. She went upstairs and changed into jeans, tall black leather boots and a green silk blouse. A black leather bag and a light-weight gray wool jacket completed the outfit. She left the house in time to arrive at precisely 1:00 as planned. Shane Anderson was already there looking over the broken wrought-iron fencing surrounding the property. He was trying to line up the front gate when he saw her arrive.

"You're right on time," he said.

"And you're early. I like that. I've been looking at your plans for the house and I like what you're suggesting. I have a few ideas of my own that I'd like to discuss with you. Shall we go in or shall we talk about the yard first?"

"The yard is the least of our problems. We can clean up the overgrown vegetation, repair the fence, prune or pull down the trees and the hard part will be done. It will only remain to replant some new flowers and shrubs. The lawn has been neglected, but there isn't a lot of the weed growth that I would have expected. I think we should get the advice of a professional for the planting unless you have a green thumb."

"Me? No. I know what I like and I can see certain plants in the beds, but planting them will have to be someone else's responsibility. I know a gardener who can make magic happen, but we need to have someone take out what's here. What about that man we met in the pub? Didn't he say he was a landscaper?"

"Yes. I still have his card. I'll ask around and see if he's the best person for the job, and if I get some good reports I can give him a call."

"Great. He had the look of someone who really needed a job. Let's go inside the house and look around."

They started in the basement and worked their way up. "I understand you plan to have certain artists giving lessons in this building, and I was thinking that maybe the basement would be a good place for a potter's studio and class room. If students drop gobs of clay, the cement floor down here would be easier to clean than the hardwood floors in the upstairs rooms. There are more windows here than you would normally find in a basement so light would be good, and if you wanted an outdoor kiln, these stairs would lead right to it. We could put a concrete pad on the ground nearby for it. The stairs would also allow clay and materials to be loaded easily down a ramp. We could get someone in after we clean it out and finish the wall, someone who might even be the person who will be working down here, who can tell us what would be needed. We'd be able to customize the space with the right tables, shelves for storing clay and completed pieces. There's a washroom with a sink and toilet in the back under the stairs, so we could bring the water out through the wall and put in a large sink. I think this would be a great space for that. What do you think?"

"I agree. I'd like to see this stairway looking a little safer. It's made of wood and it has been here unmaintained for a long time."

"Agreed. And that's an easy fix. The outside stairs can be remade as well. Shall we go up?"

"Yes. Now, on this floor, I was wondering if the walls on the right side could be removed to make a large teaching room. They aren't load bearing are they?"

"They are supporting the upper floors. It's alright though. We can reinforce them with laminated beams and close them in with wood. We can make that look original to the house, and make a large open space on this side of the building. It can go all the way back to the kitchen. On the other side of the house we can do the same if you want."

"I'd like to have the two front rooms opened up into one on the other side, but I'd like to leave the last one before the kitchen wall for an office. And there is a washroom and laundry at the end of the kitchen."

"When I told you that appliances had been removed from the house I was referring to the washer and dryer among other things."

"I would like to actually have a washer and dryer there for the towels and other things that might need to be washed. There's no need for instructors to tote those things home to wash them. Maybe we can replace the ones that were stolen with one of those sets with the washer on top of the dryer. They don't take up as much space and we won't need oversized appliances for a few towels."

"Done."

"I see that you've cleaned up quite a bit. The pictures showed a mess in here."

"When we spoke yesterday and you said you wanted me to do the job, I sent some of my men over to take away as much of the trash as they could. They cleaned out the basement and this floor. Anything that seemed like it could be saved is out in the garage. There isn't much of that sort of thing. They took away 32 bags of smelly garbage from there. I think they might have attracted some of those four-legged critters you were concerned about, so until we take care of that problem you might want to avoid the garage. It seems that your grandfather was using that building as his personal dump. We sent several truck loads to the land fill. I'm afraid there wasn't time to do the same for the remaining two floors, so we will be stepping into a big mess up there, but this will give you an idea of what it will be like when we've had a little more time."

"Thanks for that. The next floor then?"

"After you."

7

Going up the stairs and into the first room on the right was like stepping back in time. It had been her grandmother's room and Anna could remember spending many nights here and sleeping in her grandmother's huge bed with her. They would stay up until late at night talking. Her grandmother would tell her stories about when she was a little girl. Anna loved her grandmother more than anyone else in the world and when she died Anna was devastated. Then to add to the loss, her grandfather wouldn't let her come to visit. He wouldn't even let her come over after the funeral to get something, anything of her grandmother's as a keepsake. She didn't want her jewelry or her china; she just wanted something that smelled like her. Her hairbrush would have been enough, but she was denied entry into the house and she never saw her grandfather again until he was hospitalized for gall bladder surgery many years later. Her mother refused to pick him up and take him home, so the job fell to Anna. She barely recognized him after so much time had passed. He was frail and shorter than she remembered. When they arrived at his house he refused to allow her to see him inside. She never saw him alive again.

The flowered paper was hanging off the walls and the draperies were gone, rods and all. The closet doors had come off their hinges and the carpet was buckled and filthy. The smell was horrible and Anna realized that there was nothing left here of her grandmother. The other rooms were in a similar state. Anna needed to let go of her memories and get on with it. "I'd like to divide this floor the same way as we did the one below. I remember a full bath in the front of the house which we will need, but we should open up the rooms and have one long space on each side. Will that work?"

"Yes. That will work well. No problem. I don't know how you will feel about the top floor. I told you the room was sealed. Your grandfather wanted to make sure that what was up there would remain there. We opened it and, well, I think you need to see it for yourself. Shall we?"

Anna was a bit unnerved at this warning so she allowed Shane to go up first. When she got to the top of the stairs she was unable to speak. Her grandfather had made a shrine to her grandmother. Her clothes were hanging in an open wardrobe. Her china was stacked in a cupboard. Her dressing set with her comb, brush and mirror were laid out on her vanity table. Anna recognized her jewelry box and her evening purse as well as art work, glassware, things that had meant so much to her grandmother. It was all there and it caused a myriad of emotions to rise to the surface. It occurred to Anna that the reason her grandfather wouldn't allow her to take a memento was because he couldn't bear to part with anything of hers. That knowledge somehow changed Anna's attitude toward him. Shane said, "When we saw this we felt that we shouldn't touch anything. We will transport it to your home for you, though, if you'd like us to."

"I'd like that very much. Thank you. I think I'll go now. Just bring it all to me at this address," she said handing him her card. She started to go and then turned back and said, "I appreciate the way you protected all of this for me."

"I could tell by the way you spoke about your grandmother that these things would be important to you. I have some help standing by and I can have this packed and delivered this afternoon. I'd feel uncomfortable leaving it here over night since we have unsealed the door and there has been so much looting here in the past."

"I'll be going straight home and can let your men know where to put all of it. Thank you again." She went down the stairs and out to her car quickly so as not to allow Shane to see the emotions that were welling up inside her.

A short time after Anna arrived home, the truck pulled into the driveway and up to the front door. Anna was surprised to see Shane following in his own car. She instructed them to follow her to a small all-purpose room on the third floor of the house. There was nothing of great weight except for the china which she had them leave in the dining room to be put away later. The rest was easy for Shane and his men to carry upstairs so that she could take her time going through boxes of treasures. And after she thanked them and showed them out the door, she returned to the third floor and spent the rest of the afternoon reliving many childhood memories.

At about 6:00 she heard Carl calling her name. She responded and he joined her on the third floor. She had her grandmother's things spread out all over the floor. She had picked a few things to take to her room and left the rest for later. She explained it all to Carl and then they went to the dining room for dinner.

"Have you finished with the work emergency?"

"Almost. I know I promised you that I would tell you all about it, but you're going to have to wait a few more days until it all plays out. Then I promise you'll get the whole story. For tonight, I'd like to think about just about anything else. Tell me about the house and what you've decided to do. Then we can get some sleep. Remember that we have to get up early and head over to Sarah's for a day of riding horses and forgetting all about work and other people's problems."

"Alright, as long as you can promise that it is someone else's problem and not ours. I've been a bit nervous about that."

"I can tell you that it has nothing to do with us. Now let's hear about your project and how you came home with your grandmother's belongings."

8

Sunday morning Anna and Carl woke at 7:00. They had wanted to wake up earlier, but they would still have plenty of time to get to the pre-ride brunch. They showered and changed into their riding clothes and went down to the stables to get their boots and their horses. Robert knew that every Sunday the horses had to be ready to go. If they needed to be trailered he was notified ahead of time. The ride to Sarah's estate was short and so the trailer was not necessary.

Anna's horse Gallant was a bay Irish Sport horse about 16 hands in height. Ebony was of the same breed and height, but he had a black coat that was so shiny that Anna could almost see her reflection in it as she rode by Carl's side. The two horses were geldings of even and affectionate temperament. Riding them on a Sunday outing was a joy.

So was the breakfast. After everyone had eaten and had their glass of champagne, they set off out the stable gate and headed for government land. Carl took the lead. Normally it was the host who led the group, but Sarah was still uncomfortable leading onto land that was relatively new to her. So off went Carl, and Anna joined her friends Sarah, Fiona, and Bridget for the ride.

They caught each other up on what had happened to them since the last ride. That meant Sarah told about the funeral and the gathering after, and her inheritance from Mr. Ahern which had been his ornately carved wooden cane with the brass top. Bridget told about her latest fight with her husband, Fiona told about the company dinner she and her husband Charles would attend later that night at the Gentry, and Anna told about the project at her grandfather's house. She also talked about the top floor shrine to her grandmother and the fact that she had finally gotten what she had wanted for years, something by which to remember her.

Near the end of the ride when they had all told their respective stories, Sarah broke the news that the other three couldn't believe. She was going to the states to visit her cousin. That wasn't shocking in itself; the shock was that she was going to be gone for over two weeks. When they heard that the three pulled up their horses in unison. "What?" they all said, also in unison.

"I know. I will miss two Sunday rides and I know that is unheard of, but my cousin is having a personal crisis and she needs me. We were like sisters growing up and I haven't seen her in a long time, but she is going through a divorce and her kids want to stay with their father and she's in distress. I'm going to go with her across the country. We're going to go from landmark to landmark and have a bonding time and then I'll come home. It's something I feel I have to do. I'll miss all of you and this place so much, but I'll be back before you know it. I leave in the morning and since we're back at Braunleaven and I have guests to see to, this is good bye. I'll get in touch with each of you as soon as I get back."

They exchanged horse-back hugs and then she rode off as they told her they would miss her and to have a safe trip.

"Well, that's a bummer," said Fiona.

That sentiment was echoed by the other two as the day's ride was almost ruined.

9

By Wednesday of the next week work was in full swing in Anna's house and she stopped by in the morning with her camera to check on the project and take pictures to show to Carl and Fiona. The house and garage had been completely cleared of debris. The biggest difference was that the place was clean which meant it was easier to see what the end result would be. Anna and Shane roamed through the house and looked over the progress that had been made so far. The top floor had undergone the most drastic change. As Anna walked through the one large open room she found the balcony that she remembered at the rear of the house. She believed that it would provide a view of the hills beyond, and would make an excellent place for landscape painting. She took several photos at different angles to see exactly what the artists might see. Of course, the yard was a jungle with overgrown trees and creeping vines and debris. The fence that Anna remembered was totally obscured by vegetation, but that was an easy fix.

She had a clear vision for the house. The basement would make a perfect place for pottery classes. The ground floor would make a nice spot for the stained glass classes so many people seemed to enjoy these days and would not require heavy sheets of glass to be carried either up or down the stairs. The floor above could be used for photography and specialty classes with the two rooms running from front to back. And the top floor would be for painting. It was an open space in a square shape that would allow easels to be placed around the outside. It also had glass doors and a balcony that would be useful for landscape painting. The empty room that occupied part of the ground floor with the office at the rear of it could be used for a variety of things. Meetings could be held and items made by students could be displayed. There could even be a small warehouse for the materials students would need for their respective classes. She would make that decision later. She would have at least two computers in the office and she wanted the classrooms to be equipped with computers and projectors for the instructors to not only tell their students how to do things, but to also show them with video.

Anna was pleased to see that without a thick coating of dirt and dust the house appeared to be in excellent shape. Shane said that there had been issues with the plumbing that had been easily handled. "Any house that sits empty for a period of time will have plumbing issues. The water that came out of the faucets at first was dirty, but we let it run for a while and it cleared up. We'll have it tested, but it is village water so I think it will be alright. I recommend that we replace the commodes, though. They seem to work fine but they had water sitting in them for years and they can't be completely cleaned."

"Certainly. I'm pleased that we can use all the washrooms. It is important to have one working on each floor. I guess from what we see here that most of what we have to do is cosmetic."

"Yes. This house was built well to begin with. That makes it easy. I'm afraid it also means I'm not going to make a bundle on this job. It's good news for you, though, because the estimates I gave you are a bit high. What about the garage? I thought it would be useful for storage from time to time."

"I agree. If the room on the ground floor is going to be used for different purposes such as meetings, the garage might be a good place to store extra chairs and tables. As long as we can rid ourselves of those uninvited guests that had taken up residence there," she said with a smile.

"We've made progress in that area already and we'll fix it so that we can keep them from coming back."

"Good. I guess I'm going to have to start finding instructors so they can give us some input on what goes into their classrooms."

"There is one thing I wondered about. Did you hire that guy from the pub to do the yard work?"

"Of course not. I don't even know how to contact him. He gave his card to you. Besides, I wouldn't hire anyone without first discussing it with you. Why do you ask?"

"I drove by here last night. I was in the neighborhood and wanted to come by since people have been helping themselves to things. When I got here I saw a truck going in the opposite direction. Then this morning I thought I found where someone had been trimming that big tree to the right of the garage."

"That makes no sense. If he's going to do that wouldn't he rather wait until he's getting paid? And if he's not going to get paid, why would he do it at all?"

"I don't know. I think I'll call him and find out if you don't mind. Whether he thinks he can get the job or not, doing it without permission is at least trespassing, and if he tried to take the wood away that's theft, even if we don't have a use for it ourselves."

"I'd actually appreciate it if you would. Of course it might have been someone else entirely. We may find out that he had nothing to do with it. I can't tell you how happy I am with the progress so far. This is great. I'm going to possibly bring some people around to see the work spaces, but I'll let you know ahead of time to make sure those spaces aren't torn apart on that day. And so I'll go and let you get back to work. Thanks again and we will keep in touch, yes?"

"Yes, indeed."

Anna decided that as long as she had her camera with her she would go around to the side of the garage and take photos of the tree. She found it to be a large tree half still standing and half on the ground blocking the pathway between the garage and the fence around the property. It looked to her as if someone had tried to take down the tree but had realized that it would be dangerous to the building to take it down without cables and people with ropes on the ground. She wondered if someone had been trying to take the tree for fire wood. If they wanted the tree, all they had to do was ask, though whoever it was might not know that. Anna was just glad they didn't keep trying to cut it until someone got hurt.

She drove home and let May know she was going to be home for lunch and then she went to the study to check her emails. She still used email even though some of her friends laughed at her for it. She didn't want to put her business on Facebook or Twitter and she had no interest in the mindless social media posts. So she used email, though she sometimes went days without checking it. She sifted through some of the junk that she got each day, and found something from Sarah. She had written it just before she left for the states.

> *I was thinking last night about your arts center. I think I told you that we just hired a new vintner. He and his wife are living in one of the Braunleaven cottages. She taught pottery in the states before they moved here. Call the estate line and dial extension 505 if you want to talk to her. I've seen some of her work and if she is half as good at teaching as she is at making pottery, then she'd be a real asset. Her name is Ava Clark. I have to go now if I'm going to catch my plane. I'll let you know as soon as I get back. Good luck with your project.*

As soon as Anna finished her lunch she gave Ava Clark a call and made arrangements to meet with her that afternoon. She drove to Braunleaven not to see her best friend, but to meet with Ava. She had never visited anyone in the employee cottages before. She was directed by Deklin, one of Sarah's trusted employees, to go left from the stable gate and toward the woods where she and Sarah often ride. "There is a small road marked by a pair of woven-wood posts," he said. "Turn left there and go to the last cottage on the left." She'd seen the decorative posts many times and knew they marked the road to the cottages, but she had never been on it. Sarah always felt that to go riding on the staff road would be an intrusion. Anna turned left and aimed for the last cottage on the left.

She knew from what Sarah had told her that there had originally been twelve of these stone cottages, but they had been extremely small and had dated back to the building of the estate. Henry Braunlea's grandfather had built wooden additions to join each pair together. The result was six attractive cottages, three on each side of the road, identical to each other except for the color of the wooden portions and the trim on the windows and doors. What Anna saw was a lovely cul-de-sac of homes with large back yards personalized by the people who lived in them.

The last one on the left was decorated with lovely clay wind chimes and planters. When Anna used the antique wrought iron knocker, Ava answered the door. She had received an email from Sarah telling her that Anna was going to contact her so she invited her in and offered her a glass of lemonade. When Ava went to get their drinks Anna looked around at the interior of the house. She saw more examples of Ava's work and was thoroughly impressed. What she saw amounted to works of art. When Ava came back with a tray of lemonade and snacks, Anna explained what she was working on and Ava became excited.

"I'd love to be involved. It would be wonderful to be able to plan it the way I'd like and customize it to my needs. I've only worked in places that were already set up beforehand. There was always one thing or another that I would have changed if I could. This will also give me something to do with my time while my husband is working. Running this winery is time consuming. I don't want to complain; this is a wonderful opportunity and my husband loves his job, but before we came here I was busy myself. Since we arrived I've been a little bored. If Sarah recommended me to you then I can be certain that we will work well together. I am very excited about this."

Anna gave her the dimensions of the basement and the location of the wash room and the stairs, both inside and out, and told her to draw up a plan of what she would like for a studio and said that she would take her to see the space as soon as the contractor gave her the clearance. She gave her Shane's email address for her to correspond with him. They said their good-byes and Anna drove home satisfied that she had checked one instructor off her list. She had a personal recommendation from her best friend, she had seen the caliber of her work, and she had a good feeling about her as a person from their brief meeting.

It was time for dinner by the time she got home and there was a message from Carl saying that he would not be home until late. So once again she settled for dining alone, but before she went to bed for the night, she went to the third floor and spent an hour looking through her grandmother's things. There were so many memories associated with her and with her house. Anna couldn't help but wonder how her grandmother would feel about what she was doing. She knew that the house had been a source of pride for her and Anna felt a certain amount of guilt about not moving into it herself. But Kellenwood was her home and she loved it the way her grandmother had loved the house on Liffey. In a silent promise to her, Anna vowed to take care of the house and make it into something her grandmother would love.

And with that she turned out the lights and went to her own room where she read for a short time until she fell asleep.

10

Anna had lunch planned for Thursday with her friends and after dressing in cream colored slacks and a brown sweater, she tied a Burberry scarf around her neck and drove in the direction of the Gentry Hotel. She found a spot in the parking garage and handed her keys to the attendant. She walked the one flight of stairs to the lobby and remembered the first time she had ever come here. She and her grandmother came one day for high tea. They had worn party dresses and white gloves. They had held out their pinky fingers when they held their cups, and they laughed about waiting for the queen to come and join them. It was magical. After her grandmother died, her parents didn't have the money to dine at the Gentry, so it wasn't until years later that Carl had brought her here for dinner. They had ordered the cheapest food on the menu, and they drank water with their meal, but it was a real treat, and when their dessert arrived, Carl proposed to her. Now she and her friends came here at least once a month for lunch, although this day they would be one short with Sarah on her trip to the states.

She entered the dining room and found her friends immediately. They had ordered a bottle of Braunleaven wine. "May I make a toast?" asked Fiona. "Let's raise our glasses to Sarah, who isn't here in body, but she is here in spirit. Get it? It's her wine, so she's here in spirit."

"I thought we had a rule against bad puns," said Bridget.

"And if you have to explain it, it really is a bad pun," said Anna. The three of them got caught up with what was going on in their lives, and when it came to Anna she told them about the status of her pet project.

"About that," said Fiona, "I had a strange call from an old friend about it."

"Is something wrong?" asked Anna.

"I don't think there's anything wrong really. You probably aren't aware of this, but the older people who share the fence at the back of your property are the parents of a friend of ours. They lived in a big beautiful country estate, and when their son Ian got married they signed it over to him and bought the smaller house behind your house on Liffey. They are vacationing in France right now, but Ian goes over every couple of days to check on it. He went there this morning and he said that he could tell right away that someone had driven into their backyard and had tried to remove some of the sections of wrought iron fencing. He was hoping it wasn't the people working on your house, but he can't imagine anyone else doing it. He asked me to have you call him about it. He isn't angry really. He just wants to find out what's going on and he doesn't want it to happen again. Apparently his parents are obsessive about their garden."

"Okay, this is weird. I didn't tell you, but someone tried to remove the tree by the garage. I wonder if it's the same person. I can assure you that I will get to the bottom of this. There is no way anyone on Shane's crew would trespass on the neighbor's property."

"I'll go with you to talk to Ian if you want me to. I just can't do it tomorrow."

"Thanks, but I'll get Shane to go. He can assure Ian about his crew."

They finished their lunch, and on the way home Anna drove by the house on Liffey, but they had had a long lunch and by the time she got to the house the crew had gone home for the day. She would have to deal with it tomorrow.

Carl got home from work early for a change, and since it was a couple of hours until dinner, they changed and went to the stable to saddle up and go for a ride. By the time they returned it was time for dinner. They ate in the sun room and talked about the events of the day. When Anna told Carl about the tree and the fence he became worried. "I don't like this. One incident might be a fluke or somebody just fooling around, but two incidents in two days means someone is up to something. I can almost understand someone trying to steal the tree for the wood, but messing with the fence makes no sense at all on its own. I can't go with you tomorrow; we have some big shot clients coming in from out of town, but I want you to promise me that you will take Shane with you to check it out."

"Don't worry. I'm feeling a little nervous about this myself. I will call Ian in the morning and set up a time to meet and then I'll ask Shane to go with me."

For the first evening in a while, Anna and Carl had nothing on their schedules. After a scrumptious meal prepared for them by May, they were at a loss for something to do. Carl walked over to where Anna was sitting, kissed her on the neck and suggested that they should go upstairs and discuss his idea for how they might pass the evening.

He took her hand and led her up the stairs to spend the first quality time together in what seemed like a very long time.

11

Anna awoke when Carl got up to go to work. He kissed her on the forehead and wished her a good day. As he was leaving the bedroom he said, "Be careful with this trespassing business. If there's another incident you might consider calling in the garda."

"I agree. But let's keep a good thought. Maybe there's a logical explanation and we've been worrying for nothing."

"I'll see you for dinner unless the clients want to go out to eat. I hope not. I'd rather spend the evening the way we did last night."

"Cough in their faces. They won't want to share a meal with you if you're sick. And I promise dessert here will be much sweeter than in some restaurant."

"Stop it or I won't be able to go to work at all. See you tonight. If I have to stay late I'll call."

"Bye, Love."

When Carl left, Anna got up and took a shower and fixed her hair and make-up. She dressed to go out to the house in a pair of skinny jeans and a dark blue silk over-blouse. A pair of espadrilles and her hobo bag completed her casual house-renovating attire. She waited until she had eaten breakfast to call Ian Wentworth in case he wasn't an early riser. When he answered she told him who she was and why she was calling. She also assured him that no one working on her project would have trespassed onto his parents' property. "I would like to go and look at it with my contractor though, if you don't mind. We've had a similar incident on another part of that perimeter. Could you meet me there this morning or is this a bad day for you?"

"I had planned to go and check the house about 10:00 this morning anyway. I'd be glad to meet with you at that time so we can figure out what is going on."

"Good. I'll see you then."

Anna had about an hour and a half before she was to meet Ian. She spent some of that time looking at more of her grandmother's things. There were some boxes that she hadn't had a chance to break open, but she felt that judging by the speed with which she had gone through some of the other things, that an hour and a half wouldn't be enough time to go through a whole box. She opened instead one of the vanity table drawers and sat on the floor looking at pictures of her entire family taken when her grandmother was still alive. There were pictures of trips to the beach, of picnics in the park, of family dinners and holidays, and at the bottom of the stack, there was a photo of the two of them at the Gentry Hotel having high tea. It brought tears to Anna's eyes. She had forgotten that her grandmother had asked the waiter to take their photo. Anna decided that this one would be framed and hung on the wall in the bedroom. There was a small spot that would be perfect for it. Anna would be able to see it when she opened her eyes in the morning.

As she reached for another stack of pictures she caught a glimpse of her watch. She should have left ten minutes ago. She reluctantly stood, got her purse from her room and left the house. She always gave herself extra time so she was sure she wouldn't be late, but she did drive a bit faster than usual and she pulled up in front of the house fifteen minutes before she was to meet with Ian. She found Shane, explained what had happened, and the two of them drove in Anna's car around to the other side of the block for the meeting.

Ian was waiting in the driveway when they arrived. He walked over and offered his hand first to Anna and then to Shane. When all the introductions had been made, he started to tell his story. "I knew that there were renovations going on in the Kindrick house and I knew my friend Fiona was a friend of yours, Anna, so I called her about this. I come over every other day to check on my parents' house while they're away. I water the plants if they need it, I check to make sure there isn't anything requiring immediate attention in the mail, that sort of thing. Yesterday when I drove in I saw tire tracks leading around the side of the house. My parents would have a fit if they saw them. Both of my parents are extremely fussy about their garden. I just hope we get enough rain so that those tracks disappear before they return. Anyway, I followed the track all the way back to the fence. When I got there I noticed some scratching on the fence as if someone had used a tool of some kind to try to pry the pieces apart. Come with me and I'll show you."

He led the way around the side of the house to the garden. Anna had brought her camera with her and she took photos of the tracks that had been made in the grass. They continued on until they got to the fence. She took photos of the scratches and then as she leaned down to check closer, she noticed something else unusual. "Did you see that someone has planted some climbing vines on the other side of the fence?"

Shane said, "They might not have been planted. Those vines grow wild all over in untended yards like this."

"I know that, but these have been planted. Look at them. They are in a straight row all along the other side of the fence and then they turn toward my house. These were planted to cover up something. But they're so thick now that I can't see what they're hiding." Then she remembered something. "You know, I think I remember there being a shed here. If you look closely through the stems close to the ground you can see wood boards. These plants are so thick that the building has been completely obscured." She turned to Ian and asked, "Have your parents ever said anything about a shed back here?"

"Yes, as a matter of fact I do remember them talking about all the brush and overgrown plants in your grandfather's yard. They said the only good thing about it was that it hid that old shack that was in the corner of the yard. That has to be the one they were talking about."

At that point Shane said, "I think we need to check out this shed from the other side of the fence. Mr. Wentworth, I assure you that none of my people is responsible for this intrusion and I further assure you that they will never come onto this side of the fence. In addition to it being illegal, there is simply no good reason for us to do it. All of our work will be done within the confines of the backyard over there. But you have brought to our attention a mystery. I am going to drive by in the evenings from now on and if someone is doing some mischief maybe I'll catch them at it. If not we'll let the local garda know to keep an eye on both these properties."

"Thanks. I appreciate that. Listen, all of this aside, I think it's great that you're fixing this place up a bit. It's been an eyesore in the neighborhood for a long time. When my parents moved in here the house and the grounds were beautiful. The flowers were so well tended. Your grandmother used to spend hours working in her yard every day. She also had professionals come in and do the heavy work so it would always look well maintained. It was sad to see it go into a decline the way it did. It also encouraged animals to take up residence. So I know when my parents get home they are going to be delighted about it. And this issue with the fence may be totally unrelated. I just felt that the timing of it coincided with your work and it was worth checking with you. I'd appreciate it if you would keep me informed. If you find out what happened here I'd like to know about it."

"I promise you that I will."

Shane and Anna decided that before they did anything else they had to get to the back of the yard and see what was being hidden inside that shed.

Anna asked if Shane had had a chance to check with the man from the pub to see if he had had anything to do with the events in the yard and he admitted to having let it slip his mind. "I'm sorry. I'll do it as soon as I can."

"It's fine. We might as well wait now until we see what's going on with the shed."

"I'll have my men clear a path so we can see what's in it. It'll take a while so if you'd like I can have them do the work and I can call you when and if we figure out what's going on."

"That'll be good. You have my phone number, don't you?"

"Yes, I do."

12

Anna decided to tell Carl about the new developments in person. She drove to his office and parked her car in the lot next to his building. She entered through the front door and took the elevator to Carl's floor. There was an unusual amount of activity in the office. Anna wondered if this was related to the emergency that had taken so much of Carl's time lately, and then she remembered that this was the day that clients were coming in from out of town. She thought that maybe this was not a good time to show up at his work, so she turned and headed back toward the elevators when she heard him call her name.

"I'm sorry. I forgot that this was the day you had people coming in from out of town. I just remembered when I got here. I was going to leave without bothering you."

"Don't be silly. I have been wanting to know about what happened at the house. Let's go to my office and you can tell me all about it." He took her arm and led her to the corner office in the building. As he passed by his receptionist he asked her to bring in two cups of coffee. "Alright. What happened?"

Anna told the whole story as far as it went. She told him that Shane was going to call her when he had cleared a path to the back of the yard.

"I don't know why, but I just have a strange feeling about all of this. I can't put my finger on it, but I think you have first the situation with the tree, then someone tries to get to the back yard through the neighbors' yard, and now some bizarre plantings. These are odd individually, but all together they are more than a coincidence. They are kind of scary. I wish I could go out there with you today, but I just can't. Promise me that you will let your contractor take charge of this. I don't like the thought of you going out there on your own."

"I told you before that I have no wish to take this on by myself." At that moment Anna's phone rang. It was Shane. He said that they had discovered something that she needed to see. It might be nothing, but since she would know what her grandparents might have owned she could possibly solve the mystery.

"I'll be right there. I'm about 15 minutes away." She told Carl that it looked as if maybe there wasn't such a big mystery after all by the sound of it.

"Still, I'd like to know what you find out. Call me when you can."

"Will do. Bye Love."

When Anna got to the house on Liffey Street, there was a pathway cut out of the grass in the back yard allowing her to walk back to where the workmen were chopping the climbing vines that had concealed the shed. They were almost finished clearing the vegetation and they had a pile of branches and leaves that would take several truckloads to haul away. The shed had been exposed for the most part, but they intended to clear out all of the vines before opening the doors. Anna stood back to watch from a distance, not wanting to be nearby if the shed was home to rodents or other four legged critters.

"We're trying to get the shed doors open, but we've been able to look through the spaces between the boards and we can see a car in there," said Shane as she approached.

"A car? That makes no sense," said Anna.

One of Shane's workers pulled at the door on the left and another pulled at the door on the right. Both doors were imbedded in the sod that had grown freely around the shed for many years. Just when they were about to go for shovels to dig a path for the doors, one of them started to give. Nails holding the vertical boards to cross pieces on the inside gave way and the door fell apart. Inside was a surprise. A light blue car, probably about fifteen years old, was resting on four flattened tires. It was covered with a blue tarp that had all but disintegrated. Shane told Anna that it was okay to come closer and then he told her that the shed just contained her grandparents' car.

"That's impossible. They sold their car years ago."

"Are you sure? Maybe you just thought they sold it and instead they just put it away back here out of view."

"No. I had to pick up my grandfather at the hospital because he had sold his car some time before his operation. When he needed to go somewhere he hired a driver." She looked inside at the car parked there and said, "I have never seen this car before. Their last car was dark gray."

"I'm not sure what to do about this. Should we call the garda or just haul it away?" asked Shane. "It's your shed so it's your call."

Anna asked them to give her a minute while she called Carl. He felt strongly, and she agreed, that she should call the garda and that she shouldn't even touch the car. So that's what she did. She was told that someone would be out right away to see her. Less than ten minutes later the group assembled outside the shed saw a garda officer following the pathway toward them.

"Garda Simms," he said offering his hand to first Anna and then Shane. "I understand you have found a car that doesn't belong here. Is that correct?"

Anna and Shane explained the circumstances concerning the tree, the neighbor's fence and the oddly planted vines. They explained that they were investigating the contents of the shed when they found the car.

"And you've no idea who might own this car?"

"None at all. This is not the car my grandfather drove."

Garda Simms stepped forward, pulled the tarp off the car and opened the rusty doors. The inside of the car showed the effects of several years of neglect. Mice and spiders had taken up residence and some of the upholstery had been degraded. Garda Simms looked in the driver's door and immediately pulled his head out nearly bumping it on the door frame.

"There appears to be a large amount of what could be blood staining the seat," he said. "And you've never seen this car before? It couldn't belong to someone your grandfather knew, could it?"

"The reason we called you is that I don't know whose car this is. It has apparently been hidden in this shed for a long time. I'm concerned about this. It seems to me that someone put this car here without my grandfather's knowledge. He or she or they clearly wanted it hidden or they wouldn't have planted the vines to camouflage it. And now that we're renovating, whoever it is wants to get it out of here."

"I think you might be right. If someone stole the car or used it to commit a crime then they might not want it to be found. So I'd say this shed is now a crime scene. I wish I could have gotten some photographs of what it looked like before you tore it apart."

"I took photos before the vines were removed and I also took photos of the car when the shed was opened. You can certainly have them," said Anna.

"Thanks. I'm afraid my superiors would have been upset if they knew I had missed that step. But how was I to know?"

"Yes, well what now?"

"We'll want to pull this car out of here. How would you feel if we were to remove that tree that has fallen to the right of the smaller building by the house? That seems to be the only way for us to get a vehicle in here big enough to haul it away."

Anna and Shane looked at each other and came to the same conclusion. "About that, I think that whoever tried to take that tree out of the way might have had the same idea. We didn't know about the car at the time, but now that we do it seems as if someone was trying to get it out of here. This house had been neglected while Mr. Kindrick lived here alone and since his death it has been empty for a while as well. As soon as we started to work, whoever hid the car must have come back to try to get it out," said Shane.

"I don't suppose you took photos of that, did you?"

"I did," said Anna. "I'll put all the pictures on a thumb drive for you."

"I appreciate that. I'm going to take note of the plate number and see what I can find out about the owner. Then I'll arrange for a car carrier to come and I'll have to get someone here to take down the tree."

"We can do that for you. It'll be out of the way before your hauler gets here," said Shane as he motioned to his workers to get going on it right away.

With several men working on the tree, it came down quickly and Shane used his truck to pull the limbs out of the way. When the hauler arrived, the driver was able to back into the yard down to the shed, hook chains to the bumper of the car, and drag it onto the truck taking a good portion of the shed with it. As much as they might have wanted to clean up the mess, garda Simms was there to put crime tape around the wreckage of the shed. "We need to comb this area. We'll put a tent over it to keep out the weather and we'll check for any evidence of who put the car here. I'm afraid that your workers won't be able to come back here until we give you the all clear."

"Can we still keep working on the house itself?" asked Anna.

"I don't see why not. Just stay at the house and not back here."

"Thanks," said Anna as she left the yard to consult with Shane about what to do next.

"And also," said Garda Simms, "Let me know immediately if you find any more suspicious activity around here."

"We will."

13

It was lunch time and Shane suggested that he and Anna go to Kerrigan's pub, not too far from the house, to have a sandwich and chips. The proprietor delivered their food in quick time and they got right to deciding on the next steps. "I don't see any reason to allow this to interfere with the work we planned to do on the house. While this job is much easier than I had anticipated and is therefore going much quicker than I had thought it would, I still would like to keep going and move on to the next project as fast as I can. I don't mean by that that I intend to short change this job in any way; I just mean that the next project is always as important as the present one in my line of work."

"I understand."

"Also, the people who had actually been in line ahead of you have decided to reconcile and they want to get to work on their house as soon as possible."

"Listen, I never would accuse you of cutting corners for the sake of time. I have seen what your crew has done so far and the transformation in the house is wonderful. I also can understand how the other people are feeling. Garda Simms has given us the go ahead and we weren't planning on getting to the yard work until the house was nearly done anyway. So I say let's just get on with it. If any reason develops for changing our plans we can deal with it when it comes."

"Agreed," said Shane as he lifted his glass of water to toast the arrangement.

When they had finished their lunch Shane returned to the work site and Anna went home. She had planned to go through some of her newspaper and magazine articles to hunt for possible instructors for the arts center. She came across a man who had done some amazing things with stained glass. He was a bit of a self-taught artist. He had taken a beginner's course in glass work and had gone on from that humble start to winning national competitions in both stained glass design and construction. His architectural work included the replacement of a 40 foot window in a small church in Wales. He might seem to be out of the reach of a burgeoning arts center, but Anna knew from the several interviews she had done with him that he was a local person with a sense of responsibility to his neighbors and an interest in helping others learn his craft. She also knew how he appreciated the instruction he had had early on and thought that he might be just the right person for the job. And if he had no interest at all, it still would do no harm to try. He might even be able to help her find a suitable substitute. So she found his number in her contact information and dialed him right away. Waiting wasn't in her nature.

"Hello. Cranston here."

"Hello, Mr. Cranston. My name is Anna Kelly. You probably don't remember me, but a bit over a year ago I did a series of articles for the *Graent Gazette* on you and then a free-lance magazine article as well after you won the Dublin National Arts Award for stained glass design."

"Yes, I do remember. Your articles brought me so much work I had to turn some away. I appreciated that when I wasn't working myself to exhaustion. What can I do for you? I hope you don't plan more articles."

"No, I have something else in mind. I wonder if I could arrange to meet with you about a new project of mine with which I believe you can help."

"That's intriguing. Can you give me a hint?"

"I'm afraid that if I tell you about it over the phone it will be much easier for you to say no. If I keep you interested until we meet, I think I can be more persuasive in person."

"I've just left St. John the Baptist in Blackrock where I am working on a small replacement window. Would you like to meet somewhere between here and Graent?"

"You have to go very near to my home to get from Blackrock to Graent. I'll give you my address and you can join me for some of my housekeeper's cranberry scones and tea. Does that fit into your schedule?"

"Cranberry scones and tea always fit into my schedule. I will see you shortly."

She gave him detailed instructions on how to get to her home and signed off saying she was looking forward to talking to him. When Connor Cranston arrived half an hour later he complimented Anna's home as being one of the most beautiful he'd ever seen. "I love the way you've complemented the design of the house with the furniture and pieces of art that you have selected. The overall effect is stunning."

"Ah well, if I'm to be honest I cannot take credit for most of it. My husband and I bought it furnished and since we thought it was just about perfect as it was we left it alone. My American friend uses the axiom, 'If it ain't broke, don't fix it.' We didn't think it was broken. I can say that some of the art pieces are my choice. Some of them are the result of what I learned as an art columnist; some are actual gifts from the artists I interviewed. Perhaps you'll recognize this lovely stained glass egg as a gift you gave me after I interviewed you."

"I do remember. I see you've given it a place of prominence. I can't help but wonder if you brought it out of a cabinet just for this meeting," he said smiling.

"If I did my own housecleaning I'm sure I would be able to pick this up and show you the marks in the dust from where it has sat since you gave it to me. Alas, I have a housekeeper who keeps this place spotless, so I can offer no proof."

Just then May carried into the sitting room a tray of tea and scones and put them on the table between the two extra-large sofas. "May, would you please tell Mr. Cranston here how long that stained glass egg has sat on the mantle?"

"It's been here about a year I'd say, Mrs. Kelly."

"Did I at any time prompt you to say that?"

"I beg your pardon, Ma'am?"

Anna and Connor both laughed at her reaction and when Anna explained the joke May laughed as well.

May poured the tea and handed each of them a cup. "Now, I believe I have been quite patient. You must tell me why I am here," said Connor.

Anna explained all about the arts center she was planning. She started with her experiences as a journalist reporting on the local art scene, she told about inheriting her grandparents' house, and she finished with a bit of hard sell about the contribution he could make. She said that she remembered from her talks with him that he had been an older beginning student in a class and then took his art to a higher level on his own. She felt that he would therefore understand what the students in his classes would be experiencing. When she finished her pitch, Connor Cranston responded with one word, "Yes."

"That's it? I don't have to beg or plead?"

"I have been wondering why there wasn't something of this sort in Graent for some time. There are places to go to learn some things, like painting for example. People can take elementary courses at colleges and universities around here, and there are individuals giving lessons in their homes, that sort of thing. But there is no place for people to go where they can be certain that the people teaching them know what they are doing and can understand the beginner. Some of the people teaching starter classes in colleges become irate or at the least condescending when they learn that the people there to learn beginning pottery aren't already proficient at it. I call it the snob factor."

"There will be no place for snob factor at this center, I assure you. The house is on Liffey Street. I don't want to take you there right now as there is still a lot of work to be done, but I would like you to see the space you will be working in soon so that you can tell my contractor exactly what you would want." She told him the dimensions of the space and as she had done with Ava Clark, asked him to draw a plan for the space taking into consideration the tables he would use, the storage space for sheets of glass of all sizes, and anything else that would be on his wish list for the space and to email his requests to Shane Anderson. "Whatever you ask for can be done while the space is still under construction. It will be easier than building the space and then having to adapt it to your needs."

"This is wonderful. I can see you have given this a lot of thought. I'll look at it this evening and get to him soon." Anna gave him her contact information as well and said that he should contact her if he had any questions or concerns.

Not too long after Connor left the doorbell rang. May greeted Fiona and escorted her to the study where Anna was looking over more articles in search of instructors. She gave Fiona an update on the two instructors that she had enlisted and then they got down to the reason for Fiona's visit. "Ian called me and said that he had gone by the house and spoken to Shane about the shed in your yard. He said that there had been a car in there. Is that true?"

"It is. The garda assumed it was my grandfather's car, but it wasn't. We are waiting for them to run the tag numbers to find out whose car it is. Add to that the fact that someone has definitely been trying to get back to that car since we started the work on the house and the creep factor rises exponentially."

"What does Carl have to say about it?"

"He wanted me to let Shane deal with it all. But now that the garda are involved I'd say Shane and I are both going to have to leave it alone."

"Good. I'll tell you what I told Ian. This is creepy and dangerous. You need to distance yourself from it."

"I can't distance myself from it and still keep working on the center. I will, however, see to it that Shane, or someone else like Carl, is there whenever I do go to the house."

"Thank you. That makes me feel much better. I had better get home. It's late and Charles is bringing a client home for dinner."

Anna noticed that it really was late and she hadn't heard from Carl. Then again she knew there was a chance he couldn't be home for dinner. Still he said he'd call. Anyway, she felt that a salad with cottage cheese and a glass of wine would suffice, and then it would be early to bed for her. She had had a rough day. She took the articles with her to bed to continue searching for instructors, but she didn't get very far before she slipped off to sleep, letting the articles fall to the floor.

14

Saturday morning Anna awoke alone in bed. Carl had slept there; she could tell from the rumpled linens on his side of the bed. He had apparently gotten in late and gotten up early. She dressed quickly and went downstairs hoping that he had not had to go in to work again today. He was in the sitting room with a pot of tea and a cup waiting for her. His first words were, "I'm so sorry that I didn't come home for dinner last night and I'm even sorrier that I didn't call. By the time we had a break it was so late that I was afraid I'd wake you. Then, of course, I was afraid you'd worry. I didn't know what to do."

"I'll forgive you just this once, but please don't do it again. One of these days I'm going to report you to the Garda as missing and then you'll be embarrassed," she said planting a kiss on his cheek. "Where did you go for dinner?"

"Oh, we went to the home of one of the young executives in the firm. I don't think you know him. His family has had money for generations and I think he wanted to show off a bit. He really did. His people put on a spread that impressed even the most jaded of prospective clients."

"I thought these were already clients."

"No. We're trying to woo them. Anyway, I got up early because you got a call on your mobile. I took it so you could sleep. It was from a Garda Simms. He said he has some information for you and he's going to be here in about an hour. I was just about to go wake you."

"Well, it gives us enough time to have some breakfast. What would you like? Remember it's May's day off so you're stuck with my cooking."

"How about a bowl of cereal?"

"Coward," she said as she got up to put together a lovely breakfast of Cheerios, skim milk and berries from Sarah's plants. Just as they finished and she was putting bowls and spoons in the dishwasher, the doorbell rang. When she got to the sitting room Garda Simms was already seated and talking to Carl.

"Good morning," said Anna as she joined them.

"Good morning, Mrs. Kelly," said Garda Simms. "I was just about to tell your husband that we have found out who owned the car we found in the shed in your backyard. It was registered to a man named Thomas Killern. Is that someone you know or someone you think your grandfather might have known?"

"I have never heard that name," said Anna. "To be honest, I did not have a very close relationship with my grandfather during the last 15 years of his life, so who he might have known and who he might not have known is something I can't tell you. Do you know anything about this person? If I knew where he was from or what he did for a living then I might be able to make some connections to my grandfather if any exist."

"We know a few things about him. He was not from here originally. He only moved to Graent about ten and a half years ago. He was employed as a carpenter generally and he did wall board work specifically. He was apparently quite good at that. We also know that he was reported missing about ten years ago. That means that he only lived here for about six months. That is going to make it hard to retrace his steps up to the time he disappeared."

"I don't understand. Are you saying that the car in my yard belongs to someone who might have been a victim of foul play?"

"We have to approach it that way. He was reported missing by a young woman who said she hadn't seen him in about 24 hours. She said he had left Kerrigan's pub the night before in an extreme state of inebriation, and she was worried that that had been why he was missing. We can't even take the report until someone's been missing for 48 hours so she was sent away. The garda on duty was new and he didn't even write down her name. A few days later he was reported missing by his employer and the search was on for him and for the woman who reported him first. We never found either of them. We started to think that maybe the two of them had run off together, but since we never got her name, we had no way of finding that out."

Carl asked, "What will you do next?"

"This is a weekend and we're a small force. We have our only forensics team out looking over the shed and so we put the car in the impound lot. We'll go over it with a magnifying glass on Monday to see what we can learn. In the meantime, there is something else to report."

Just at that moment the doorbell rang again, and May showed Shane into the sitting room. Anna made the introductions between Shane and Carl and Shane said, "I guess Garda Simms here has told you what I came to talk to you about."

"Actually, Sir, I think I was just about to. You see, Mr. and Mrs. Kelly, last night after our crew went home for the evening, someone set fire to the shed. There's nothing left of it."

Anna put her hands over her mouth and Carl got up to go to her. "Please tell me the fire was limited to the shed," she pleaded.

"Yes, it was. The fire was started from inside the shed and it looks as if the person who started it wanted to ensure that he didn't draw the attention of the fire squad. He brought a hose and ran it from a spigot on the outside of the house to the shed and put the fire out as soon as the shed was destroyed. The wood was so old that it went up rather quickly. The fire was reported by a neighbor, but by the time the trucks got there the fire was out and the person who had set it was gone. He left the hose as if he had to leave in a hurry. I doubt that we'll find prints on it. I'm sure he was being careful. We'll try anyway."

"Did the firefighters see anything?" asked Carl.

"No, but they were concentrating on putting out a fire, not looking for who might have set it. The fire is always their first concern."

"Understood."

"How is it that you came to know about this, Mr. Anderson? Is your crew working on a Saturday?" asked Simms.

"We were. I sent them to pick up some supplies when I got there and found out about the fire. It's the sort of thing that they can do until we feel that it's alright to go back to work. As I explained to Anna yesterday, we have another job that was actually supposed to have been done before this one. It had to be postponed, but the clients want to get started now as soon as possible. That's why we were working on this job on a Saturday." Shane explained about the divorce that didn't happen.

"If you don't mind, Sir, I would like you to suspend work for the day. I know that will be inconvenient for you, but there is something fishy going on there and we need to get to the bottom of it. I promise that my men will work as fast as they can to gather evidence. It's always crucial with an outdoor crime scene anyway. I'll let you know when you can go back to work."

"I'd appreciate that."

"I'm so sorry Shane," said Anna.

"That's alright. I'll see if I can meet with my next clients and get some of the prep work done. It will actually be good because I can find out what materials I'll need and order them. That way they'll be delivered during the time I'm working on your project. Just let me know when I can start up again."

As both Garda Simms and Shane were about to leave, Anna reminded Simms that she had a thumb drive with photos on it for him. She went to the computer and ejected the drive. She returned to the sitting room and gave it to him and asked to be kept informed as much as the law would allow.

15

Carl and Anna were both stunned by the accumulation of the events of the last few days. "I have an idea," said Carl. "Let's go upstairs and take a shower, together," he whispered in her ear, "and then we can decide on what to do for the rest of the day."

"I totally agree with the first part, the shared shower."

They took a long time and while they were toweling off, Carl said, "Let's go for a ride."

"Horse or car?"

"Car."

"Where do you want to go?"

"We get in the car and we drive. We leave the mobiles off and we just drive, just you and me. When it gets to be lunch time we can find a place to eat, and then we'll come home a different way and find a place for dinner. It's May's day off so that's a great excuse to not stay home and cook. We've both been busy and things have been stressful. I think we should turn off our mobile phones and go. What do you say? Shall we do it?"

They had already released much of the stress of the last few days, and the relaxing drive relieved even more. They didn't use the GPS, and they didn't go to familiar places. Anna said, "I have an idea. We'll alternate left and right turns. Of course if a right turn takes us to a steep cliff we can turn left, but otherwise we follow the right/left rule and see where it takes us." And so they did. They drove for hours, stopping at antique shops where Anna found some interesting pieces of porcelain, and for Carl, a retro leather pilot's jacket. He was a handsome man already, with sandy brown hair and brown eyes, and a fit body on a six foot frame. The jacket just gave him an extra dose of cool. She looked at him and said that the jacket was made for him.

They stopped at a greasy roadside stand for fish and chips, something Anna rarely indulged in, and then they turned and drove on toward home. For dinner they did a bit better. They found a beautiful old mansion that had been converted into a top-rated restaurant and had a wonderful meal there of steak and mushrooms with potatoes cooked in cheese. Carl loved his beef and he pronounced it among the best steaks he had ever eaten. He reached across the table when the server asked if they wished to order dessert, and he said, "I think we'll have dessert at home." When the waiter had left them alone, he kissed her hand and said, "Sorry if that embarrassed you, but I'm just feeling so in love with you I don't care who knows."

"It's hard to be angry with you for that. Let's go get some dessert."

As they drove toward home Anna felt that they had reconnected. Carl had been among the missing for some time and she had allowed a bit of doubt to creep into her thoughts, but after this lovely day she felt so much better. How could she have doubted him? She took his hand in hers as he drove and felt completely at ease. Whatever problems Carl was having at work, and whatever new issues might arise in connection to the arts center or to the mysterious car in her grandfather's back-yard, they would deal with them together.

16

The next morning was Sunday and that meant getting up early for a day of riding. Anna had her alarm set, but Carl woke her up early with kisses. She started to get out of bed and he pulled her back with urgency. Half an hour later they shared a shower and then dressed in their riding clothes. They grabbed a quick snack on their way through the kitchen and headed for the stable. The ride today was at the home of Harvey Glavin, an older gentleman who had been one of the founding members of their riding group. He lived over an hour away by horse, so they would use the trailer today. Robert Callahan had their mounts blanketed and their legs wrapped for the ride and Carl's Range Rover was hitched to the trailer. The saddles and bridles were in the trailer tack room and they had only to load the horses. When they were in place Carl and Anna got into the vehicle with Carl in the driver's seat.

They arrived at Harvey's home half an hour later where they unloaded the horses and led them to stalls in the stable. Often when they trailered to other people's homes for their rides they had to tie their horses to the end of the trailer with a hay bag between them. At Harvey's the stable was large enough to accommodate several of the horses on the ride because his stable was large and because Harvey had fallen on hard times and he was down to one horse from a herd of up to 50 at one time. They had arrived in time to claim two stalls and they settled their horses into them and went to the house for brunch.

Harvey was one of a long line of family members who had inherited the estate and had sold it off bit by bit to keep the home running for one more generation. Harvey was a widower. His wife had died many years ago and they had never had children. This took the pressure off of Harvey and his feeling was that as long as he could stay in his home until he died, he was okay with selling off works of art, collections from previous generations, land that could be taken from the outer edges of the property. There were rooms in the house that had not been occupied in years. Why did those rooms need valuable works of art when they could be sold to support him in his old age? What he was living on now was the income from those sales. And why not?

Carl and Anna joined other riders for the walk to the house. Upkeep on the house had suffered during the last several years and what had once been manicured gardens were now mowed flat for minimal maintenance. The water features that used to dot the grounds were turned off and their fittings had rusted closed. The larger of two stables that had once held part of his herd of horses had fallen to the ground and the remains had never been carted away. But when it was Harvey's turn to host the ride he used the resources he had left to put on a magnificent spread. He hired day workers to prepare the food, set the tables with the best of what he had left for silver and china, and serve his guests their food and champagne. When the meal was over the guests walked to the stable to find their horses saddled and bridled and ready to go, and their trailers were swept out and refilled with clean shavings.

When the call came to mount up, the trays of champagne were brought out by waiters and each rider took a glass. They toasted the ride and the host and replaced the glasses. Harvey led the group out to government land for a day of riding in beautiful weather. Anna found Bridget and Fiona waiting for her and they all felt a bit incomplete without Sarah there. They caught up with each other's lives and of course Anna told them all about the situation at the house.

"This is another reason why Sarah should not have gone to the states. She would have been able to solve this mystery in, what does she call it? A New York minute."

"I don't think Sarah would tackle this. She solved a 30 year old mystery with the help of official records. This is a current case and is being handled by the garda," said Fiona.

"Yes, and there was no sign of illegal activity going on in her own back-yard. I think that makes a big difference. If I were you I would stay away from that place until they find the person responsible for the fire. He or she may be trying to cover tracks. You could get in the way and it could get dangerous. Even Sarah was held at knifepoint," said Bridget.

"I promise to be careful," Anna said. "I am not as brave as Sarah and I don't have her detecting skills. I'm leaving this to Shane."

"Ooh, Shane the contractor. Is he good looking?" asked Fiona.

"Does he wear one of those tool belts?" asked Bridget.

"Okay. Let's talk about something else," said Anna, and they did. They visited for the duration of the ride and said their good byes before driving off toward their respective homes with their respective husbands. They got home after Robert had turned in for the night, so they unloaded and unwrapped the horses, led them to their stalls, and unhitched the trailer. They walked to the house and found the sandwiches that May always left for them in the refrigerator after a Sunday ride. They opened one of the bottles of wine that Sarah had given them. After they ate Carl headed for the study to make some phone calls and Anna went upstairs and revisited her files about artists in search of a painting instructor. She tired fast and before Carl came upstairs to bed she was fast asleep.

17

Monday morning Anna woke about 8:00 to find that Carl had left for his office. She spent a relaxing hour with a breakfast of toast and jelly with tea, and she read the newspaper in the sitting room. At 9:00 the phone rang and May brought it to her. "Hello, this is Anna."

"Mrs. Kelly, this is Garda Simms. I have some news for you."

"What is it?"

"Remember that I told you that we would start going over the car this morning for evidence. We began that investigation and when we opened the trunk we found something disturbing."

"What?"

"We believe that we have found the body of Thomas Killern."

"What?"

"We believe that the night that he disappeared he was actually killed and placed in his trunk. He was then probably driven to your grandfather's shed the same night. Now we have to find out who's responsible."

"Garda Simms, this is disturbing to me. We have had someone trying to take down a tree to make a pathway back to that car, when that didn't work that person tried to get to the shed through the neighbor's yard, and after we found the car he or she burned the evidence to hide a murder. I'm a little frightened by what that might mean for any of us who work around that house," Anna said.

"I understand that Mrs. Kelly, but since the car and the evidence are now gone I would expect that the danger to others, if there was any, is gone now. Also, all of those attempts were made when the person knew that there would be no one on the site. We will certainly give your yard some attention for a while until we can be sure that you will be left alone. I do think that you should let your workmen know about our findings, though. They ought to have the option to not work there. In fact I can tell your contractor about it if you'd like. I'm on my way over there now to close down the crime scene and remove the tape. Would you like me to do that?"

"I would appreciate that. Please tell him to contact me if he needs to discuss it with me. And thank you. I don't know how much you're allowed to tell me about the ongoing investigation, but I would appreciate it if you could keep me informed. After all, I do have an interest in what you find."

"If there is anything that I feel I can disclose I will let you know. I will also tell your contractor when he can resume work."

"Thank you very much."

Anna hung up the phone and sat immobile in her chair. She was stunned. An attempt to create an artistic outlet for the people of Graent and the surrounding area had just turned sinister. She started to have doubts about the entire project. Just as she was wondering if she should abandon the idea and sell the house, the phone rang again and it was Fiona. "Anna, I have the best news. I went to a party last night for the executives at Charles' firm and there is a new member whose wife taught painting up north before they moved here. I told her about your arts center and she is really interested in talking to you about doing some teaching. She doesn't need money so she would do it strictly on a volunteer basis. And, another attorney heard us talking about it and he said that his father had just come here to live. He's a retired professional photographer and is totally bored with retirement. He thinks his dad would love to be involved."

"Fiona."

"I talked to him about it a lot and he said the walls in his father's house are filled with covers from all over the world that he's done for magazines. The woman I told you about has had her own shows at galleries in Dundalk."

"Fiona."

"I think I've found you two good prospects, but you don't very excited about it. You're welcome."

"I have had some other news this morning. They found a body in the trunk of the car they took out of the shed in my grandfather's backyard."

"Oh, my God! Whose body?"

"His name was Thomas Killern. He was the owner of the car and he was reported missing about ten years ago. I don't mean to sound ungrateful about the instructors you found for me, but I'm a little rattled. I feel like I should put this project on hold."

"Why? The car's been taken away hasn't it? Doesn't that mean that the danger is gone, too?"

"That's what Garda Simms said."

"Listen, I understand why you would be upset. What has Carl had to say about all of this?"

"He has gone to work. I got the call and as soon as I hung up you called."

"You sound like you need friend therapy. Let's meet at Kerrigan's pub for lunch. I have some things to do this morning near there, and I can meet you at 12:30. Does that work for you? I'll call Bridget and tell her, too."

"That sounds like exactly what I need. I'll see you then."

"Good. And don't worry."

When Anna hung up she called Carl and got his voice mail. She left a message for him to call her on her mobile. She explained that she would be going to lunch with Fiona and Bridget. Then she went upstairs and showered, fixed her hair and make-up and dressed in black skinny jeans, black knee high boots and a gray cashmere turtle neck sweater. It was understated for her, but she didn't feel like bright colors on a day when she had had news of a murder, literally in her own back-yard. She didn't need to rush and by the time she went to the garage to get her car and make the drive, she had enough time to pull into a parking space directly behind Fiona.

18

Fiona met Anna on the street outside Kerrigan's pub. She told Anna that Bridget would not be able to join them. "It's just the two of us. No Bridget, no Sarah. It feels strange."

"This whole day is strange. And a drink would taste good. Let's go in."

They walked toward the back of the pub to the only empty table in the place and ordered chef's salads and house white wine. It came quickly and they settled into easy conversation about the center. As they talked the other patrons filed out one table at a time as lunchtime came and went. They both ordered coffee and pie so they would be able to justify staying put. As they were just about to finish Anna saw Garda Simms walk in and approach the owner, Teddy Kerrigan. He asked Teddy if he had ever heard of Thomas Killern.

"Tommy Killern. Yes, I have heard of him. Why do you ask?"

"Do you remember him coming in here about ten years ago and getting into a fight?"

"Here's the thing. I don't remember him very well. I do remember that about ten years ago I was questioned about him because he had been reported missing. I didn't know him at all, but I did remember the fight he had in here that night. He and another fella mixed it up over a girl. It usually is over a girl, you know. Anyway, the only reason I remember is because the garda came here just two days after it happened.

There are fights started in here almost every night, but that night he and the other guy just left. The girl left with Tommy, but there was nothing else after that. When I was questioned back then I told them the same thing I just told you. I had never seen either of the two men before that night and I never saw them again after. I had seen the girl, but I never knew her name. What's this about? Why are you asking me this again after all these years?"

"I'm not really able to go into that. Here's my card. If you remember anything about that night or about Thomas or Tommy Killern, give me a call, will you?"

"Sure, but I gotta say, if I haven't remembered it after ten years, I don't see much chance of me coming up with anything new at this point."

"I realize that. But just keep the card and if you remember anything, no matter how insignificant it might seem, just let me know."

"Did you hear that?" whispered Anna. "This is where Thomas Killern was last seen before he was stuffed into the trunk of his car. I should go and talk to Teddy."

"Whoa Anna. You were just talking about how afraid you were because of the dead body in your yard, and now you want to get involved in a police investigation. I don't think that's a good idea."

"I'll just go and ask him about it. What can that hurt?"

"Did you ever stop to think that maybe he's the one who killed that guy? You don't know anything about any of these people except that one person is dead and whoever killed him is still alive and well right here in Graent. You need to be careful."

"I will." Just as Anna started to leave her seat, a woman about 30 years old came out of the kitchen and spoke to Teddy. It was clearly his daughter. She wanted to know what the garda wanted and her father told her.

"I remember that night," she said. "He and that other guy were fighting over the girl who was in here for the good-bye party. They all left within minutes of each other. I wonder why they're asking about it now."

"That's what I said, but they wouldn't tell me."

"That's how I can get them to talk," said Anna, and with Fiona trying to grab her arm to stop her, she got up and approached the bar. "I'm sorry to insert myself into your conversation, but I can trade information about the reason why the garda are asking if you can give me information about that party. My name is Anna Kelly. I hope you don't mind my intrusion, but I have my own reasons for wanting to know about that night. Can we make that trade?"

Teddy and his daughter looked at each other and it seemed that his curiosity outweighed his skepticism. "You first," he said.

"The garda have not told me that this is a secret or anything, and so many people were there when this all started, that it's going to get around anyway. Tommy's car was found in the backyard of a house that I just inherited. There's more to the story, but I think I really should keep that to myself, but the fact that they found his car and he had been reported missing, has them asking questions about that night."

"After all this time they found his car?"

"I had started to renovate my grandfather's house and the person who hid it there tried to get it out before we found it, but he or she failed. Now what about that party?"

Teddy's daughter Una said, "There were several people here saying good-bye to a young woman who worked with them. She was moving to Scotland to go to university. Most of the partiers left after they gave her a going away gift, but she and two others girls stayed on and had a few drinks. Then Tommy came in and one of the girls went to the bar with him. Then the other fella came in and eventually got into it with Tommy."

"Can you tell me where these people worked?"

"Yes, I think I can. I remember that Donny Colligan's mother was with them. She used to manage that clothing store that was by the bridge on the high street. It isn't there anymore, but Donny's mother works at *Oldies but Goodies*. That's an antique store down near the church. She might be able to tell you about who those girls were."

"Thank you for the information. If I may give you a bit of advice, I don't think you should tell anyone about the conversation you had with me or with Garda Simms. If the person who tried to retrieve that car were to hear about it you might be in danger."

"Ms. Kelly, I have been working in this pub my entire life. I inherited it from my father and my daughter here will inherit it from me. If we were to repeat every conversation that took place in here we would quickly be out of business. People like their bar tenders to keep their mouths shut. That's what we do."

Anna and Fiona left the pub and drove in their separate cars to *Oldies but Goodies*. Before they went in they pretended to window shop while they decided on a plan of action. They decided that they would pretend to be customers and Fiona would at some point claim to remember Mrs. Colligan from the clothing store and that would give them their lead in. When they walked in a small bell tinkled in the doorway. A woman who appeared to be in her late sixties greeted them and asked if she could help them. They said they were just looking, but that she had some lovely pieces.

"Thank you. I haven't seen you in here before."

"No. We just heard about the store from friends. They were right, too when they told us how nice the store is."

"Are you looking for something in particular?"

"I would like an umbrella holder. Do you have anything in an old one that's still in good condition?" asked Fiona.

"Not at the moment, but I am getting the estate of an elderly gentlemen next week and I did notice an umbrella holder in his entry. It was brass and in perfect condition. It should be here by next Friday at the latest. I can put it aside and you can come in and look at it."

"I appreciate that. You'll forgive me I hope, but you look so familiar to me. Where have I seen you before? Did you work somewhere else before you came here?"

"I did. I worked at the used clothing store down the street until it went out of business."

"That's it. I remember now. I used to take items in there to sell when I cleaned out my closets. There were three young women who worked there who seemed to be good friends. They were nice. What happened to them? Are they working around here somewhere, too?"

"Oh, I know who you are talking about. We used to call them the Three Musketeers. They were such fun together. One of them moved to

Scotland to get an education and never returned. We had a party for her when she left. One of the other ones, poor thing, was killed a week later. It was a terrible mugging."

"That's horrible! What about the third girl?"

"She's still around here. I've seen her just recently. She's going to have a baby soon. Isn't it funny how one minute everyone is happy and content and the next one dear friend has moved away and another is dead? Taryn and I were talking about that very thing when I saw her."

"Taryn? That's an unusual name."

"It's an old name, but I've known several Taryn's."

"Do you remember her last name?"

"No, I'm sorry I don't."

"What about the other two? What were their names?"

"The one who moved away was Jenny or Jessy or something like that. The one who died was Margaret. Margaret Connors. She was the one with all the personality. She was so much fun. The boys all loved her. She was such a flirt."

Anna spoke up at that moment and said, "We've taken up too much of your time. Perhaps we should go now and come back next week when the umbrella holder might be here. Should we go now Fiona?"

When they got outside of the store Fiona said, "What do we do now? We have names now that we can use to locate the other people in the pub that night. What's our next move?"

"The last I knew you wanted me to give it up. Now you want to go looking for strangers."

"I think we should start with the computer. We can find the articles from the papers about the mugging and there might be something we can glean from them."

"I'll do that when I get home."

"Okay, but would you consider going to see the painter I've found for you?"

"Yes. If you had asked me earlier I would have definitely said no, but now I think I can manage to concentrate on something other than Tommy Killern. Lead the way and I will follow."

They arrived at the home of Kate Adams. She answered the door as if she were expecting them. She invited them in and offered them a cold drink. They both accepted and she brought lemonade and sugar biscuits and placed them on a glass top table in a sunny breakfast nook. There were paintings scattered around the house in a variety of styles. They included simple portraits, landscapes, seascapes and still-lifes. Anna was no expert, but she knew what she liked and she liked Kate's work. They got right to it and Anna explained the purpose of her center and what she expected of the instructors who were to teach there. She asked Kate as she had asked the others, to use the dimensions she provided and draw up a wish list for her space. She gave her Shane's email address and said it would be easier if she sent her request directly to him.

Fiona had to leave in time to get ready for dinner out, but Anna and Kate continued to discuss the opportunities the center might provide. Kate seemed so interested that Anna offered to take her to see the place.

"I'd love to see it. That would be wonderful."

"Let me call my contractor and see if it's in condition to be seen."

Shane felt that it would be fine to have Kate see her space and so they left immediately in Anna's car. When they arrived Anna introduced Kate to Shane and then escorted her to the top floor. Kate pronounced the space ideal and began at once to decide how she would use it most effectively. Anna went downstairs and found Shane.

"I gather Garda Simms came to see you today and told you the news," she said.

"Yes. We were all a bit shocked to hear it. He assured us all that the danger had been taken away with the car, but he wants us to be on the lookout for anything that might be considered evidence."

"There's not much chance of that after all these years, unless we find something that was left when the killer tried to cut the tree."

"We probably destroyed anything like that when we moved the tree ourselves. Anyway, work goes on. I feel like we've made good progress."

"I agree. It looks better than I had imagined it would."

"Not only is the space beautiful, but I will get plenty of exercise going up and down those stairs," announced Kate as she descended the stairs.

Anna delivered Kate back home and headed for Kellenwood. It was dinner time when she arrived and May told her that Carl had been home and eaten a sandwich and left again. He also said to tell her not to wait up for him.

Anna felt as if this had been going on long enough. She was going to have a talk with Carl. Things were going on in her life and she needed his support. She wasn't one of those wives who demanded her husband's attention at all times. In fact she felt that she was quite understanding of the demands of his work on his time. But the least he could have done would have been to call her or leave her a voice message. But the day had been a difficult one. She would have her dinner and go to bed. She would deal with Carl later.

19

Tuesday morning Anna awoke to the phone ringing. It was Fiona. "Good morning. Did you get a chance to find out about the girl who was killed?"

"No. I got home late and didn't have the energy. I took Kate and showed her the center and she seemed to like it a lot. Besides, it was probably just a coincidence. How was your dinner?"

"Boring and fabulous at the same time. The clothes were the fabulous part; the conversation was the boring part. How about you? You don't seem very chipper this morning."

"I don't know what to think about Carl."

"What's he done?"

"He hasn't done anything really. It's just that he's either here wanting to have sex or he's gone. There's never anything in the middle. He wasn't here last night. He had been and gone when I got home. He left no message for me and he is gone already this morning. I'm sure it's nothing, but I feel like he's keeping a secret and he's never done that before. He said it was something at work and he would tell me about it when he could, but I don't know if I believe him."

"You need to get out of the house and get your mind off of him. Let's go and meet our photographer. I saw his son again last night and he's mentioned it to him and I get the impression that he's excited about it.

I'll go and pick you up in an hour and a half and we'll drive to his house. We can plan the rest of our day from there. How's that?"

"That sounds great. I'll be waiting."

Anna dressed in jeans and sandals with an oversized pull-over Irish knit sweater. With all the troubles she had on her mind she felt the need to be comfortable. Fiona arrived right on time as always, driving her Audi convertible with the top down. Anna usually cared more for her hair than for fresh air, but on this day she tied her hair back with a barrette and let the wind blow in her face. The trip to Jacob Terrier's house was a short one. Fiona had called ahead so he was expecting them. He lived in a converted coach house made of stone. It was covered in ivy and had flower boxes in the front windows. The yard around the house was mostly grass and well maintained, but there were vibrantly colored flowers in corner beds. Anna imagined him taking pictures of those flowers.

"Please come in," he said. "You have no idea how happy I was to learn about your project," he said as he pumped Anna's hand in a shake. He was a kindly older man with white gray hair and lively blue eyes. He wore tan corduroy trousers, leather slippers, and a plaid shirt tucked in at the waist. He looked like someone's grandfather and that made Anna think of her own and the shrine he had built to her grandmother. She couldn't help the smile that spread across her face and into her eyes. She liked this man the way she believed Sarah had liked Braden Ahern.

"When I retired from photojournalism, it was because the stress of traveling became too much for me. I remember thinking when I made the decision that if I had the chance I would like to pass along what I know to others. If you will allow me to participate in your venture I will be extremely grateful. But first I imagine you want to see if I know what I'm doing. Am I right?"

"I'd love to see your photos. Please." Anna and Fiona followed him into a small sitting room the walls of which were covered with his pictures. It was an eclectic collection of war scenes, natural beauty in far-away places, color, black and white, sepia concept photos, and faces young and old, animal and human. Anna didn't know where to rest her eyes. "You're an artist," she said. "I will be one of the first to sign up for your class."

"Wonderful."

"I have found someone to teach pottery, stained glass, painting and now photography. I gave each of the others the dimensions of their rooms and asked them to put together a wish list. I'd like you to do the same thing and email your requests to my contractor. Will you be teaching digital photography or film?"

"I can teach film, but my sense is that most of your beginning students will be more interested in digital photography. It is much more accessible to people who have a computer but not a dark room."

"I agree. If you want computers in the room or a projector or anything of that sort, just put it all on the list and we will get it for you."

"I think a computer and projector for me would be good, but is there money in the budget for the students in the class to have computers as well?"

"There is. We had planned on spending more on the renovation than it looks like we will have to so there will be money for extras."

"In that case a photo quality printer would be great."

"Done. And there is a closet in that space large enough to add a dark room later on if it's needed."

"Let's take him to the house," said Fiona.

"I'd like that. I'll go change from slippers to shoes and be right back."

When they got to the house the workmen were dealing with plumbing issues. Anna and Fiona led Mr. Terrier up to the second floor area which had been designated for his classroom. He liked the space and felt that he could teach quite comfortably there. They decided not to interrupt Shane's work and left for Jacob's cottage. When they arrived he promised to put some ideas for the space on paper. His enthusiasm ensured Anna that he was the right choice for the job.

Anna and Fiona then returned to Anna's house to have lunch and talk about the things that were going on in Anna's life. When they finished eating they went into the study and searched the internet for stories about a young girl named Margaret Connors who had been mugged on the streets of Graent ten years before. They found the first news item and several updates that followed and reported basically that there were no clues to the identity of the person responsible. She had been two blocks from her home when she was dragged into an alley and strangled to death. The accompanying photograph showed a lovely young woman with shoulder length blonde hair and a crooked smile. She had been killed two weeks shy of her 22nd birthday.

Margaret Connors had gone to school in Graent and went to work in the used clothing store as soon as she graduated. She had been the only child of a single mother and she had had a hard life. But she didn't let that affect her future. She enjoyed working with her friends and occasionally she allowed herself the luxury of a couple of pints in the corner pub. She had two good friends, one of whom had left for Scotland and the other who had stayed in Graent. She would be about the same age as Margaret, her name was Taryn something, and she was currently pregnant. Graent is not a big place. People knew one another. They just needed to figure out how.

But not today. Fiona had to go home. She said she was sorry that she couldn't stay with Anna since she was going to have to spend the night wondering what was going on in her marriage. But Anna wouldn't hear it. "Just because my marriage may be falling apart is no reason for you to jeopardize yours. Go home and enjoy your marital bliss. Look, I'm probably making something out of nothing. Carl will walk in here soon and tell me the whole story and it will be reasonable and logical. I'll call you in the morning and we'll talk about it."

They said good bye and Anna found May to tell her that she would settle for a sandwich for dinner with a glass of wine. She took them to the third floor and spent the rest of the evening looking at her grandmother's clothes and pictures. She found some items that represented precious memories for her. She reminisced until she could no longer keep her eyes open. She went to bed and wondered if she would be sleeping alone from now on.

20

Wednesday morning Anna decided to start fresh. By that she meant that she was not going to worry about Carl until she found out for certain that she needed to. She had to give him the benefit of the doubt since she and Carl had been together for so long without ever having had a serious argument. He had always been honest and she couldn't just assume that he was lying now. So she had breakfast and got dressed and drove to the house on Liffey Street. The first person she saw at the site was Shane.

"Good morning Anna. Come to check up on us, have you?"

"Good morning. I have indeed come to check up on what works of wonder you have performed. Are you ready for the instructor's requests?"

"I have already received several of them via email. I think that leaves just one more. I have heard nothing from the painter. That's okay though, because we have plenty to do to on the other spaces. Also, it's about time to get started on the yard."

"Have you decided yet who you will hire to do the yard prep?"

"I haven't had time to think about that in the time since the car was taken away. I do think it's about time to decide on that now, though. I will put that on my list of things to do when I get home tonight. That's the kind of thing I can do after the sun goes down."

"Doesn't your wife object to your bringing your work home?"

"I'm not married, so no."

"I'm sorry. I thought you were wearing a ring."

"I was married for three years and my wife died. I can't seem to take it off just yet."

"Please forgive me for getting so personal. I was out of line."

"It's fine. Let's just go inside and see the pottery space. We've been concentrating on it for the last couple of days. Your instructor actually came by here a couple of days ago and walked us through what she'd like to have." Anna followed him down the outside stairs and into the basement. The space had been transformed. The walls and floor had been painted white and a drop ceiling had been installed. There was a new block of shelves on the wall near the door and Shane's carpenters had created carts with wheels on them to allow Ava Clark to move heavy blocks of clay around easily. Tables had been built to her specifications and a large utility sink had been installed on the wall outside the washroom so that the pipes could be shared. Both sets of stairs had been replaced and there was generous lighting spread around the entire room. Ava had requested a computer and projector for her classes and a place had been reserved for them. The equipment had not been purchased yet, but the hook ups were installed.

"This is wonderful!" Anna said. She was so excited that without thinking she threw her arms around Shane's neck and hugged him. "I absolutely love it. With all this business about the car and the dead body, I was feeling a bit down, but this gives me an idea of what the rest of the house is going to be like and I can't wait for the rest to be completed." Anna meant nothing by the hug and went about her inspection of the space as if nothing had happened. She was completely unaware of the effect it had had on Shane.

"There's more to see," he said. He led her up the stairs to the ground floor rooms and showed her first the stained glass room with space for a custom built storage area for sheets of glass. There was a large table with electric outlets spaced along the edges for the equipment that would be used for creating glass pieces. He also showed her the conference room he had built for Anna. There was a large table in the center that had been built specifically for the space. "There are chairs on the way. They should be here shortly. I sent some men to pick them up in Dublin."

"So if I had a meeting here this afternoon or tomorrow evening there would be places for us to sit?"

"Tomorrow would be better. If you can wait the one day they'll be here."

"Then I think I will call the instructors and ask them to join me here tomorrow evening. We can talk about the schedules they'll have and an open house. I think we should have one of those. I have been thinking that for this space we should have computer capability. I can just imagine some people asking us to provide instruction on how to use computers. Would it be possible to make this table you've made computer ready?"

"That will be an easy fix. In the meantime I'll make sure that the space is cleaned and ready for your meeting before we leave. Oh, and we replaced the locks on the doors and I have a set of keys for you." He pulled a key ring from his pocket and handed it to her. "I've marked them so you'll know which ones are which."

"Thank you. Thank you for everything. I'll bet you had no idea when you took on this job that you were getting involved in a murder investigation."

"I admit that when I met you I had no idea that that would happen."

"I'm sorry for that."

"No. I haven't had this much excitement in a long time."

They discussed a few more details related to the renovation and before Anna drove out of the driveway she called Fiona and asked if she wanted to join her for lunch. She said yes and they decided on Anna's house. They also decided that Fiona would call and invite Bridget as Anna was in her car.

21

They all arrived at the same time and entered the house together. Anna went to the kitchen and asked May if she could manage two extras for lunch and she said that she could whip up something for the three of them in about half an hour. Anna took that time to tell about the status of the work spaces in the house on Liffey. Before they knew it lunch was ready and they went to the sunroom and ate while they talked about when they would get their friend Sarah back.

Anna and Fiona also told Bridget about everything she had missed in the case of the body in the car. They told her that they had learned about a person named Taryn, but they did not know her last name. "Taryn is not an uncommon name, but we can narrow it down by her approximate age," said Bridget. "I have a friend who has worked at the school in Graent for about 25 years. She can probably tell you the last names of all the Taryn's who ever went through the system. I'll call her."

While Bridget was on the phone Anna and Fiona discussed the possibility of calling Garda Simms. "Let's wait and see if Bridget can find out anything for us and then we'll decide," said Anna.

Just then Bridget said, "I'll be back in about 20 minutes." With that she was gone.

"Well, what was that all about?" asked Fiona.

"I guess we'll find out in about 20 minutes. In the meantime, has Charles ever kept secrets from you?"

"Charles is an attorney. He has to keep secrets. Sometimes I think it is second nature to him. I'll tell him sometimes about something that happened to someone we know and he'll say, "Yes. I would have told you, but I didn't want to reveal any privileged information. I tell him that the person involved is not a client of his and he'll say he knows. It's just force of habit."

"You know what I mean."

"I do, but here's something else I know. Carl loves you. He couldn't keep that a secret if he wanted to."

Anna felt a bit relieved and she and Fiona talked about nothing important until Bridget returned. "I think I have what you're looking for," she said putting a thin book on the coffee table between them. "My friend remembered a girl named Taryn McKenna who left school about eleven years ago. I have her school book picture here."

Anna took the book and said to Fiona, "Don't be angry with me, but this is one of the reasons why I believe that Bridget is the smartest of our group."

"Yes, she's a genius. Why didn't we consult her before? Oh, I know. She didn't want to join us for lunch on Monday."

"Couldn't, not didn't want to."

"Wait a minute. This candid photo of her next to her formal photo has someone else in it that I've seen recently. He was in the pub the day I first met with Shane about the house. When he walked by our table he saw the pictures and offered to do the yard work for us. You don't suppose he had an ulterior motive?"

"Can you find a photo with his name next to it?"

"Yes. Here it is. His name is Jack Corrigan. I remembered that it was Jack but didn't have the last name. I think that maybe we should take this to Garda Simms. But I've just had an idea. Before we do that maybe we should take it to the pub and ask Una if she recognizes Taryn and Jack. Does anyone want a pint?"

They took Bridget's BMW and drove the short distance to Kerrigan's Pub and took seats at the bar. Una came from the kitchen and said hello to Anna and Fiona and said she was surprised that they were back again so soon. "We have something we want you to look at. Do you remember this girl?" said Anna.

Una looked up at her and said, "That's one of the girls who was here that night."

Anna showed her the picture of Jack and Una reacted the same way again. "He's the one who was in the fight with Tommy Killern. The only reason I remember is because it was fresh in my mind when the garda came here ten years ago."

"Thank you, Una. You have been a big help."

The three friends left the bar and decided a trip to the garda headquarters was in order. It wasn't far and when they arrived Garda Simms was just leaving the building. Anna ran to catch up with him and asked if he had some time to talk about the case.

"I have a little time. I'm just on my way to Kerrigan's to see if they remember anything more about the night Tommy Killern was last seen. I'm trying to get a line on the other people involved. You'll have to make it fast, I'm afraid."

"That's why we're here. We may have some information for you. I was in Kerrigan's when you went in to talk to Teddy. My friends and I go there sometimes for lunch. Anyway, I found out from Una after you left that the girl that Tommy and the other person were fighting over was there for a going away party. We also learned that she used to work at the used clothing store by the bridge and that the woman who now runs *Oldies but Goodies* was the manager there and had attended the party, too. We went to see her and got the name of a girl who had been there, but was mugged and killed a week after the party, which might or might not be a coincidence, and also the first name of the girl the two men had fought over. Then we found someone who worked at the local school and gave her the first name and she thought she knew who it might be. She had a class book with the girl's picture in it and we took it to Kerrigan's and showed it to Una and she said that was the girl. Then we showed her the picture of a boy who was in the girl's class and she said he was the man who fought with Tommy. I have the book and I've marked the relevant pictures."

Garda Simms looked at her as if he couldn't believe what he was hearing. "Did you take a breath while you were rambling on like that?"

"I get a bit carried away when I'm excited. Besides, you told me to make it fast. Anyway, here's the book. Also, I have met the other man. When I was talking to my contractor in Kelly's pub a couple of weeks ago this man approached us and offered to do the yard work on our renovation project. I actually thought at the time that he was overly interested in the project but I assumed that he was just in need of work. Now I think that he wanted to know what we were doing and he wanted to have access to the shed."

"You may be right. I really appreciate this information, but I have to ask you to let me deal with this from now on. There could be a degree of danger involved."

"Trust me, I am not a fan of danger. If you go to see Shane at the house he has the business card the man gave him that day. There is one more thing. The woman, whose name was Taryn McKenna, is pregnant according to the manager of the antique store."

"Thank you for that. We'll be careful if we come into contact with her. Now, really, your involvement is over."

"Could I still get you to keep me posted?"

He said he would if she promised to stop investigating, and taking the book, he returned to the station presumably to look for addresses of the principals involved. "I'm glad that's over," said Anna. "I remember how much trouble Sarah got into because she wanted to do just one more thing to help."

"You should concentrate on the center instead. I'll take you home now and you can tell me on the way about how you plan to advertise it," said Bridget. "I haven't seen any ideas for ways to let people know what you're doing. You have to start now with putting paper around in area businesses, galleries, libraries, etc."

They discussed it and by the time they arrived at Kellenwood, Bridget had volunteered to create a brochure and some signs and posters to advertise the center. Anna told her she would get pictures and brief bios of the instructors for the pamphlet. They spent some time planning what should be included and how they should be designed and then Fiona and Bridget went home. Anna sent emails to each of the instructors asking for a biography of 200 words or fewer and a current photograph so that Bridget could get started. When Bridget gets her teeth into something she does it fast and she does it well.

After she did the emailing and some other business that she had left undone over the last week, she went up to bed wondering if she would see her husband at all before she fell asleep.

22

That night Anna got a text message from Carl saying that he was sorry, but he wouldn't be home for dinner one more time. He promised that this would only go on for a few more days. By the weekend he would be able to tell her the whole story because the client in question would be out of the country. Alarms were going off in Anna's mind, but her faith in her husband was strong and he had had episodes of this sort before that involved financial problems on a scale that Anna couldn't imagine. She would talk to him tomorrow and let him know that even if he had a big issue to deal with at work he should still find the time to touch base with her.

Again she was unable to do that. He was gone before she woke up and left her a note telling her that just the opposite was about to happen. He was going to be at meetings and conferences for the next few days and might not have the opportunity to contact her. She was to plan her days and her nights without him and he would explain after the ride on Sunday. For Anna that was unacceptable and she dialed his cell phone to tell him that and it went to voice mail. She tried the same at his office and again it went to voicemail. She decided that when she planned her day as he put it, her plans would include a visit to his office.

She decided to take a horse-back ride to cool off and after her ride she returned to have breakfast and a shower. She dressed in a pair of black slacks and a red sweater with a designer scarf around her neck, and got her car from the garage. Carl usually had lunch about 11:30 and she thought she knew where to find him. She walked into the employee cafeteria and scanned the room. Carl was nowhere to be found. She walked down the maze of hallways to his office and tried to go in, but the door was locked. There was no assistant sitting at the desk outside and when she looked in through the window she saw no sign on his desk that he had even been there. The meetings and conferences he wrote about must be taking place somewhere else.

Anna was frustrated. She needed to do something and since it was lunchtime and since she sometimes ate when she became anxious, she drove down the street to one of Sarah's favorite American hamburger fast food places and ordered a cheeseburger and one of those thick milk-shakes that Sarah loves so much. She was on her way out the door when she saw Jack Corrigan entering through the door on the other side of the restaurant. She hid behind a partition and as he stepped up to the counter Anna saw the girl from the school book. Then, to Anna's surprise, she walked over to Jack and whispered something in his ear. When she went to the ladies' room Anna followed her.

Anna stood at the sink and washed her hands for a long time waiting for Taryn to come out of the stall. She said to her, "Oh my, you're going to have a baby. That's wonderful." She got no response. "Is it a boy or a girl, or do you know?

"It's a girl."

"Wonderful. When are you due?"

"In a month."

"That's exciting. I'll bet you have the room all ready, and clothes bought. That must be fun for you and your husband."

At that Taryn started to cry.

"I'm sorry. Did I say something wrong? I didn't mean to upset you."

"My husband says we have to move. I just got all my records from my doctor this morning so we can leave in the morning. I was looking forward to walking her in the park with my friends and their kids. I don't have any family but I don't see why I should have to leave. He says there's work up north and he doesn't even have a job there. I don't know what to do." She sobbed uncontrollably and Anna put her arm around her shoulder.

"When did he make that decision?"

"Just a few days ago. He came home and said that we had to move. Just like that. I said no and he said we had to. He had already told the landlord to rent our place. Now even if I say I won't move I have no place to stay."

"You're leaving in the morning?"

"Yes. We have someone coming at ten to buy some exercise equipment of my husband's and then we're going to go. Our trailer is packed and ready to hook up to the truck." The sobbing increased.

"Are you going to be alright? I can't help but think that this is too much for a woman in your condition. Where do you live?"

"We have half of a duplex on the corner of Mable Road and the high street. Why?"

"I thought you might need a ride home."

"No. My husband is outside waiting for me. Thank you for listening to me. It's my problem and I'll deal with it. I have to go." She rushed out of the room and Anna followed. She went to her car with the intention of going straight to garda headquarters. And that would have been the end of it except that as she was driving out of the parking lot, Taryn and Jack were walking to their truck and Taryn waved to her as she drove by. Anna saw Jack's reaction in her rear view mirror and knew that she had just had a narrow escape.

23

Anna decided at that point that she was not cut out for the stress that comes with trying to find a murderer. She called Garda Simms and told him about her chance meeting and that Jack and Taryn were leaving town and gave him the location of where they were living, and that that was the end for her. She was going to stop thinking about it and leave it to the professionals. She would concentrate on her pet project and her marriage and that was plenty to occupy her time. To that end she contacted each of the people she had asked to teach at the arts center and invited them to the house on Liffey to see the place and talk about where they would go from this point on. She also asked Kate Adams to bring her wish list with her. She asked each of them if they had sent their information to Bridget and each of them already had, which was good news.

The next thing she did was talk to May about what sort of thing she would suggest for finger snacks for the meeting. She then went to the market and bought everything on the list May had given her. She took the food and drinks to the house and placed the cold things in the new refrigerator and stowed the rest in cabinets. She bought paper plates and napkins as well as plastic utensils.

Before she left she looked for Shane and found him on the top floor looking out the window at the hills beyond. "It's a beautiful view isn't it?" she asked.

She had startled him and he turned around quickly and said, "Yes, it is. I sometimes come up here to eat my lunch." She noticed the chair he had placed on the balcony.

"When I was a little girl I used to do the same thing so I understand why you do it. Of course, I pretended I was Rapunzel. I don't suppose you were doing that were you?"

"Excuse me?"

"Not Rapunzel, of course. I think you were just pretending that you were King Arthur rallying his knights for the upcoming battle."

"Is that how you see me, as King Arthur?"

"Yes. I can see you as a knight in shining armor ready to rescue damsels in distress."

"Well then, my lady, what may I do for you today? Are you in distress?"

Anna didn't know how to answer that question. She was feeling a bit distressed about Carl, but she couldn't go into all of that with Shane. So she just said, "No, I just wanted to let you know that I will be having the meeting here this evening as planned. We'll be here about 6:00 if that's okay. Will your crew be out of here by then? I don't want us to be in their way."

"Yes. We will be out of here for sure. We usually leave by 5:00."

"Great. Well, I'll leave you to speak to your troops." She laughed as she turned and left the room. She had no way of knowing that he stood looking at where she had been long after she left the room.

She headed home and shortly after she walked in the door the phone rang. It was Bridget who said she had spent the entire evening and the morning as well working on the brochures and flyers for the center. She said the instructors had all emailed their information and photos to her and she had been able to incorporate them into the brochures. She proudly announced to Anna that she had a first draft ready for her. "Could you make a half dozen copies for the meeting I'm having tonight?"

"Sure. When is the meeting?"

"It's going to be at the house at 6:00. I can go by your house to get them on my way there."

"Okay. You can have the instructors comment on what I have done and let me know what changes need to be made. This is exciting. Thank you for letting me be a part of it."

"Thank you for doing this. You have a real talent for the computer stuff. I'm no good at it. I'll be at your house about quarter to six to pick them up."

"See you then."

Anna needed a shower and a change of clothes. She dressed in jeans and platform shoes with a white silk tee and a red jacket with her favorite red Celtic design scarf. She fixed her hair and put on light make-up. She found her hobo bag and her car keys and she left, not knowing if Carl would be home or not. If so, he would be the one to wonder where she was for a change.

When she arrived at Bridget's home she took a quick look at the brochure that she had made and pronounced it perfect. She had taken a photo of the house for the front panel and said that she would replace it with a new photo when the entire renovation, complete with yard work, was done. She had a panel for each of the instructors complete with a picture and brief bio. She had a panel for contact information and hours of operation, none of which could be included in the brochure's first draft. Tonight's meeting would decide those details. She wanted Anna to give her the name of the center as soon as she could so that that could be added as well. She told Anna that she was also going to set up a web site for the center that could include all of the same information as the brochures, but it could also provide members of the community with a way to make suggestions for new classes and generally give input to the people who would be ultimately making policy. Anna thanked her for everything and set off for the meeting.

The center was well received by the instructors. They conferred with each other about times that would be convenient for them as well as some of the teaching aids and materials they would need. They discussed the texts they might want students to have and wondered if they should be provided or if students should purchase them themselves. They talked about what students might do with the items they produce. Would they have a room to display items, or would they want to contact the local library to see if there might be a way to exhibit pieces there? The discussion was lively and enthusiastic and lasted longer than Anna had expected it would. In fact they didn't seem to want to leave. When the meeting was over they all left the building together and headed for their cars. The meeting had been a success and in addition to being people who would make excellent instructors, Anna believed that they were also nice individuals who would work well together as a team.

Anna waved them off and then got into her own car. Her Mercedes was new and well maintained. There had never been a mechanical problem of any kind with it. So Anna was surprised when it didn't start. She tried several times and had no luck. She tried to decide who to call and thought of Shane. She dialed his number, but before he answered there was a knock on her window. She turned and was surprised to see Jack Corrigan pointing a hunting rifle at her.

"Get out," he said. "Leave the phone in the car but bring your purse." His voice was eerily calm.

She opened her door and asked, "What do you want from me?" She was trying to remain calm but was not succeeding.

"Let's don't lie to each other. You and I both know why I'm here. We have to put an end to this."

"I don't know what you're talking about."

"Since you can't stop lying then you should just shut up. Walk to the side of the garage."

Anna felt completely alone and was feeling that she had taken the search for the killer too far. She also knew that Carl wouldn't miss her and the chances that someone would show up and save her from this man who had already killed once and maybe twice, were slim.

24

Anna was told to get into the truck that Jack had parked in the pathway where the fallen tree had been. She did as she was told and he slid behind the wheel. He reached over and took her hand and slipped it into a zip tie already attached to the bar on the headrest. Only then did he put down the rifle. "Where are you taking me?"

Jack reached out his hand and slapped her hard across the face. "I'm going to tell you one more time to shut the hell up. If you don't I will put a gag in your mouth and tape it shut. Nod your head if you understand me." Anna nodded and sat in silence as they pulled into the driveway of the home that Taryn had told her about. He drove his truck well behind the building and parked behind a small barn. He walked around the front of the truck and opened her door. He pulled a knife from his belt, cut the zip tie and told her to get out. They walked in the dark toward the back door of the house and he pulled it open for her to walk through it into an almost empty kitchen. She could see through open doorways that the rest of the house was in the same condition.

"If you promise to stay put I won't tie you to that chair." She nodded and sat down. "You have stuck your nose in my business and now I have to take my wife and move her away from her home just before she's to give birth. We would be gone already except for two things. She had to get her medical records at her appointment today, and I needed to get some money. I had arranged to sell some of our things, but the buyer can't get the money until Monday. I thought I had time to wait until I found out that you had spoken to my wife. Now I can think of only one way to get enough money for us to get away. You're going to give it to me."

"I'll give you all the cash I have, but I don't carry much on me."

"That's not good enough. You are going to be our guest tonight and in the morning we are going to go to your bank and you are going to take some money out of your account. When I have the cash, I will let you out of the truck along the road. I don't want to hurt you. I never wanted to hurt anyone. You want a beer?" he asked opening the refrigerator. She shook her head.

"You killed Tommy Killern."

"That was an accident. He fell and hit his head. There was nothing I could do to save him."

"If that's true then why didn't you just call the garda and report it?"

"I had just been tossed out of a pub for fighting with him. What do you think everyone would have thought? I would have been arrested for killing him and I would have lost Taryn forever. I couldn't take that chance."

"Why did you put the car in the back yard at my grandfather's house?"

"We had just removed the tree that fell on the old man's roof and then I heard that he was in hospital. I thought I could put the car there temporarily and move it when I figured out what to do with it. Before I knew it he was back home and I couldn't take the chance that he would see me try to move the car out again. I went back after I heard that he died, but by then that tree had fallen on the side of the garage and I couldn't get it out without someone seeing me."

"Did you put climbing plants around the shed to hide it?"

"I did. After a while I started to think that I didn't really need to move it. I thought old man Kindrick would live for years and by then I'd probably be long gone. But you know how it is. The years go by so fast. Taryn and I got married and we were so happy. I can't say that I ever forgot about what I did, but I put it out of my mind. And that's the way it would have stayed, but then I saw you in the pub making plans to renovate the place and I knew I had to leave. But pulling up stakes takes time and before I could get it all taken care of I saw that you and Taryn had talked. You got her to tell you where we lived and I knew it was just a matter of time before they came for me."

"Haven't they come here for you?"

"They have, but look at the place. We've moved out for all they know. I'm taking a chance staying the one more night, but we have no money and I need you for that."

"You seem like a nice man. I'm sure that if you explain everything then if you do go to jail it will be for a short time. You've got a child on the way. Taryn won't leave the baby's father and it's been ten years. Surely you've earned her love in those years."

He looked at her and his expression turned to anger. "You're lying to me again. You know that there's more to it than the accident Tommy had. You know about Margaret, don't you?"

Anna didn't respond. She didn't want to say that she knew, but she also didn't want to say something that he knew was lie. She felt that talking this out calmly was her key to survival. So she just looked at him and said nothing.

"Margaret Connor was a friend of Taryn's. At least that's what Taryn thought. Margaret had gone out with Tommy behind Taryn's back and she had made a pitch for me when Taryn was seeing Tommy. So she wasn't much of a friend if you ask me. She was in the ladies' having a smoke near the window when Tommy and I fought in the alley. She saw the whole thing and a couple of days after it happened she knocked on my door late at night. She walked in and said that she liked my place and that she could be really comfortable there. I asked her what she was talking about and she said she knew what I had done. She said that if she and I got married she couldn't be made to tell anyone what I had done. She said that we would have a good life together. She said that she had had a crush on me for years and that she would make a better wife than Taryn. I told her to get out. She asked if I didn't want to think about it, and I told her I would go to prison before I would marry the likes of her. She tore open the door and said I would be sorry for that. So I followed her. When she got close to her place I dragged her into the alley and strangled her. I stole her money and made it look like a robbery. Then I went home and Taryn got there soon after and she was my alibi."

"When you told me you never wanted to hurt anyone, then that was a lie."

His anger seemed to grow. "I didn't want to do it. She wasn't worth going to jail for, but she was going to ruin everything. She was going to hurt Taryn and I couldn't have that. If Taryn hadn't turned to me when Tommy disappeared, if she had told me she wanted nothing to do with me, then I would have gone to the garda myself. But Taryn did turn to me and we were back the way we were before Tommy came to town. I couldn't throw that away."

"Then you and Taryn got married."

He became calmer and more pensive. "We got married and I was so happy, but once in a while I could see her thinking of something sad and I couldn't help but think that she was wishing I was Tommy. That's why I couldn't come clean about it."

"You didn't trust me." It was Taryn who had heard it all. She walked into the room and confronted Jack. He was unable to speak. "You know it has always been you. I just went out with Tommy because you were taking me for granted. I never cared about him. He was fun and he was exciting, but I always wanted you. I knew he ran around with other women. I even knew about Margaret. She was always acting so sweet, as if she cared about me, but she was just trying to get information. When Tommy told her to take a walk, that he couldn't stand the sight of her, she decided to go for you instead. If only you had talked to me. Instead you just let me go."

He walked to her and put his arms around her and held her tight. "What do we do now?" he asked her.

"We do as you planned. We take Anna to the bank in the morning so she can get us some money and then we let her out when we're outside of town." She turned to Anna and asked, "Is that alright? You were so nice to me the other day. I really don't want to hurt you, so if you could get us some money so we can go away, then we will let you go."

"Yes. I can get you about ten thousand without any red flags going up. But I don't want to go with you in the truck. After I get the money I want to just walk away. I won't do anything and if someone asks I will say I gave you the money. And I have one other requirement."

He said, "What's that?"

"Don't ever hit me again."

"Agreed. I'm sorry."

"What about it? Will I be able to walk away after I get you the money?"

"Taryn and I will discuss that. For now you can use the washroom if you need to and then we're going to lock you in the back room. There's a mattress in there and no windows. We'll wake you early so we can get to the bank when it opens."

And so Anna spent the night trying to sleep on a single mattress on the floor with no sheets and one dirty pillow over which she spread her jacket. The room was totally dark and she could hear none of the discussion taking place on the other side of the door. Against all odds she actually got some sleep and when Taryn brought her a cup of coffee and a slice of buttered toast in the morning she ate and drank and Taryn told her that they had decided that she could go as soon as they had the money. Anna felt relieved, but also wondered if she could trust a man who had killed twice and a woman so quick to forgive her husband for two murders.

"So as soon as you get the money I can go free?"

"Yes. You know, he's a good man," Taryn said. "I know he did wrong, but he's always treated me like a queen and I love him. I've known him my entire life and I trust him. I don't know what I would do without him, especially with the baby on the way."

"I understand. I've been married ten years, too. I'm now finding out that my husband is not the man I thought he was, but I still love him. Listen to me. When you get to wherever you're going, if you need anything get in touch with me. You can find one of my business cards in my purse. If you need anything at all, including more money, we can figure out how I can help you without my knowing where you are. There are ways to do that and I have a friend who can figure it out. Promise me you will."

"I promise. Now you had better go wash up and get ready to go. Jack is getting the truck out so that as soon as we get the money we can drive off. You've been really nice about all of this. If you had been hard-nosed about it, I think Jack would have gotten nasty and he might not have agreed to let you go at the bank."

"I think you probably convinced him and I thank you for that. I'll be glad when this is over with so you can be on your way and I can get home. But I am serious about helping you when you get settled."

"Thank you. You have been great about this. You're a good person."

25

When Taryn and Anna walked out into the driveway, Jack was waiting for them. He had put a fast coat of blue paint on the white truck to alter the appearance and Anna recognized her tags on the bumper. She and Taryn went around to the passenger side and Anna helped Taryn into the center of the seat before she climbed in and closed the door. She asked Taryn if she were feeling okay and Taryn replied that she was fine, that it was just getting difficult for her to make the climb into the truck.

"That's why you're going to stay put when we get there. We don't want to have to take the time to get you back in," said Jack.

"What about the trailer?" asked Taryn.

"We'll come back and hook up to it after we have our money. I don't want to have to deal with it in case we have to run for it at the bank. I don't expect any trouble, especially if our friend here does what she's promised to do, but I think we shouldn't tow the trailer around town."

They made the short trip across town and pulled up to the bank and into the parking lot. Since they were the first customers of the day, there was plenty of space near the bank entrance. Jack backed the truck into a space so he could drive out when he left, just in case. He and Anna got out and headed for the bank. "Stay put," Jack said to Taryn as he walked away.

Inside, Anna approached a teller she had met several times in her dealings with the bank. She tried to act as normal as possible with a man with a knife standing behind her. She filled out her withdrawal form and handed it to the teller who said she would be right back. "Where's she going?" Jack whispered nervously.

"Relax. It's a large sum of money and it's early in the day. I'm sure she doesn't have it in front of her."

The teller returned, handed Anna the cash and walked away quickly. Even Anna wondered what that was about. As they started to leave the bank, security guards confronted them and told them to stop and stand where they were. Jack grabbed Anna by the arm and whirled her around to face the guards and put the knife to her neck. "If you don't let us walk out of here I'll put this knife into her jugular."

The guards seemed confused at this turn of events. One of them asked, "Who are you?"

"None of your business," Jack yelled. "Just let us go out that door and no one has to get hurt. But I will kill her if I have to."

The guards stepped out of the way as Jack and Anna backed toward the front door. When he was finally outside he pushed Anna hard to the ground, not realizing in time that Taryn was standing in the path of her fall. Anna tried to correct her position to avoid Taryn, but she had no control over her body and she landed hard on Taryn's legs. Taryn's head hit the pavement hard and she screamed in pain. When Jack saw what he had done, he hesitated slightly, and then, as if he realized how critical the injury was to Taryn, he ran toward his truck to get away. As he peeled out of the parking lot garda vehicles swarmed into the street behind him. Seconds later, as Anna was trying to get to Taryn to see if she were injured, she heard a horrible crash and saw above the vehicles in her way, a plume of smoke. Guards surrounded her and she yelled to them to call for help, that Taryn was hurt badly.

An ambulance arrived within minutes and the two women were loaded into the back, Taryn lying still on a cot and Anna kneeling by her side and holding her hand. Taryn awoke for a brief moment and asked about Jack. Anna could say nothing, but that said it all. A tear appeared in Taryn's eye and she said, "I want you to take care of my baby."

Anna started to say that Taryn would be fine, but Taryn knew otherwise. "I have no family and Jack had no family. My baby will be alone in the world. Please, I know you're a good person. You tried to help me. Don't let me die thinking that my child will be sent from one foster home to another. I beg you."

"If you survive I will help you in any way that I can. If you don't I will raise the child as if she were my own."

Taryn raised her eyes to the technicians working to keep her alive and said, "You're witnesses. You can tell the courts what I wanted for my baby." They both nodded. "Thank you, Anna," she said and then she lost consciousness.

26

After an extensive medical examination, Anna was pronounced fit to go home. But before she could leave she had to find out about Taryn. She went to the desk and asked how she could find out about someone who had been brought in with her. "I need to find out some information about the woman who was brought in in the same ambulance with me. She was in bad shape and she's pregnant."

"Let me see what I can find out for you," said the nurse on duty. She went to the counter behind her and made a phone call. When she returned she asked Anna, "Are you a member of the woman's family?"

"No."

"Then I'm afraid I can't give you information. We can only discuss a patient's condition with a member of the immediate family."

"I understand that. But she has no family. She and I were injured together and I need to know if she's alright, and I need to know if her baby's alright as well." Anna was pleading; she had to know.

"I wish I could tell you; I really do."

Just then Anna saw Garda Simms walking toward her in the hallway. She rushed to meet him and said, "I'm trying to find out about Taryn but they won't tell me anything because I'm not family. Can you tell me how she's doing?"

"I'm sorry but she died on the operating table. The baby survived, though. Poor little thing is an orphan now."

"My God. Jack died, too?"

"Yes. He died in the accident, if that's what it was. By the looks of things he drove right into that bridge abutment. What I don't know is why."

"I think I know. Not only was he going to go to jail, but he had just seen Taryn's head hit the concrete hard and he probably felt responsible for it. He had pushed me into her. I'm sure he thought she and the baby would both die and he had nothing more to live for. He really loved her and the baby was so important to him. I don't even know why she was there. She was supposed to wait in the truck. Why did the guards stop us? I took money from my own account and we were leaving the bank. I don't understand what happened."

"We'll look into that, but the sad part is that now that baby has no one."

"Not exactly. Taryn made me promise before she died that I would take the baby and raise her as my own. It wasn't a hard decision to make. I'll do it willingly."

"That's wonderful news. I have young ones of my own and all I could think about was that baby not having a home. How would I feel if that were one of mine?"

"I don't know what the legal issues will be, but I'll move mountains to get her as my own. Jack and Taryn made some mistakes and there is no excuse for murder, but I couldn't help wanting things to work out for them."

Anna walked to the nursery to see Taryn's baby, or rather her baby. She was a bit undersized because of being born a month early, but she was perfectly healthy in spite of the way she entered the world. Anna fell in love at first sight. She had thought she couldn't feel that way about another baby after she lost her own, but she was wrong. She was so tiny and helpless and as Anna looked through the glass she promised to take care of her for the rest of her life. "I'll be back tomorrow little baby. And soon you can go home with me."

She called Fiona and learned that she and Bridget had just pulled into the hospital parking area to pick her up. They both ran to her in tears as she left the building and hugged her tight.

"We have been so worried," said Bridget. "Shane said he had gotten a call from your mobile number, but you hung up. So he drove by the center and saw your car out front and no you to be found and he called Fiona's painter friend. When he learned that the meeting had ended some time before, he became worried and called Garda Simms. He also contacted Fiona, and she and Charles went immediately to the center to see what they could do. Fiona called to check with me and I hadn't heard from you. I drove to the center, too. It was Charles who discovered that the battery terminals on your car had been disconnected. We just knew at that point that there was something horrible going on. He reconnected them and gave the keys to Fiona."

"We've been looking for you all night," said Fiona. "We were worried sick, and we couldn't even find Carl to get him to help. Garda Simms called Charles and filled him in on what happened. That's how we knew where you were."

"I have to say that if Shane hadn't gone to check on you we wouldn't have known you were missing," said Bridget.

"Right. And I have to say that he didn't act as if he were just a contractor," said Fiona.

They arrived at the center and Fiona went in to tell Shane that Bridget had taken Anna home and that she was safe. His relief went beyond that of an employee. Fiona couldn't help but think that if Anna hadn't been married, she and Shane would have made a great couple. And she was feeling so angry with Carl for not being there for Anna that she couldn't help but think that, married or not, Anna deserved someone who cared so much for her. She turned to leave, but before she left she turned back and asked him, "Do you ride horses?"

"I'm Irish. Of course I ride horses. Why do you ask?"

"Oh, no reason." She drove Anna's car home, hoping that she wouldn't get in trouble for driving without tags, because they all three agreed that Anna was still too upset to drive herself.

Anna had spent the morning in the hospital, so when Garda Simms told her that he needed to get a statement from her, she asked and was given permission to go home, take a shower, and get her husband to drive her to the station at 2:00 in the afternoon. When Anna arrived home she realized that once again she would not be able to count on Carl. He still wasn't home. At a time in her life when she had needed him the most, he wasn't there for her. But her friends were. They waited for her to shower and change, and May fixed them each a sandwich and a cup of hot tea before they left.

Bridget drove Anna to headquarters, dropping Fiona at home along the way. She was to collect her husband Charles and meet them there. Charles wanted to be there as Anna's attorney, even though she was the victim and not the criminal. She told the story from start to finish and when it had been typed and Charles had read it through, she signed it. Garda Simms thanked her for her help and told her to get some rest. He said that even if she felt fine at that moment, that sometimes there was a delayed reaction to stressful situations such as the one she had been in and she might crash. "Keep someone close by in case that happens. You might need someone to talk to. Your husband, for instance."

"Yes, my husband. That's a good idea," she said sarcastically.

She and Charles left Simms' office and saw Bridget and Fiona in the waiting room. She knew that they would be the ones watching over her and not Carl. "Charles, I'm going to need to talk to you tomorrow, if that's okay. I have a legal issue to discuss."

"I'll be happy to talk to you tomorrow. But for now, go home with your friends and get some rest. Call me in the morning."

"I will and thank you for everything. You're a rock."

The three women went to Anna's and they found that Carl was still not there. They spent the afternoon telling and retelling the story and analyzing it. Anna was held at knife point and robbed of a large amount of money, which of course Jack had not had time to take from her, but she felt a degree of affection for Taryn and was truly sorry to lose her. At one point in the conversation Anna just happened to mention that she was about to become a parent.

This stunned her friends. "Do you think Carl is going to go along with that?"

"Carl is nowhere to be found. If and when he comes back I will tell him that he is going to be a father and if he doesn't like it he can disappear again."

They stayed with her the entire evening and sometime after dinner when they all started to yawn one after the other, Anna told them to go home. They made plans to meet for lunch the next day. Anna went upstairs and resisted the urge to take sleeping pills to help her get some much needed rest. She eventually fell asleep dreaming once again about talcum powder and babies.

27

Saturday morning Anna woke surprisingly early. She dressed in a pair of brown slacks and a beige cashmere sweater. She ate a hearty breakfast for her, but she had not had a real meal the day before. What passed for dinner was salad with cheese and chicken in it. So this morning she asked May for French toast and sausages and after she ate she called Charles and asked him to come over. Fiona had already told him about the baby so he knew what he was going to be asked to do. There might be some problems with the courts, but he felt that there was no better person to take care of that baby than Anna. He wasn't quite as sure about Carl as a father.

Anna answered the door and invited Charles into the sitting room and she got right to the point. "I'm sure that Fiona told you about the baby."

"Yes. Congratulations. You'll make a great mother."

"Will I? I don't mean will I be good to the child. I love her already. I mean will the law allow me to be her mother?"

"I made a call to a friend of mine this morning. He's a family court judge and he's going to do everything he can to expedite the process. How long will she be in the hospital before she'll be allowed to come home?"

"Because of the nature of her birth they want to keep her there for a week at least."

"That's good. What we don't want is her being allowed to go home before you're cleared to take her. Getting someone to say it will work is one thing, but getting the paperwork taken care of simply can't be done on a weekend. I'll go in to my office today and get everything done that can be done so that on Monday we'll be able to get started without delay. In fact if there's nothing else I'll go now."

"Thank you Charles. I'll see you tomorrow."

"Yes and I'll give you a status report then."

"Charles, I have one more question. How did the garda know that we were going to be in the bank?"

"I've been wondering that myself. I'll see what I can find out as your lawyer."

Next on her schedule was a trip to the hospital to see her daughter. She was not allowed to hold her or even go near her, because she was not considered family. She was allowed, though, to watch her through the glass and she did so for an hour. She didn't want to say good-bye, but she did and then she whispered that she would be back for her. She had to meet Bridget and Fiona for lunch and they decided to go to Kerrigan's Pub.

They met outside and walked in together. They said hello to Una and told her that when she had a minute they had something to tell her. It took her a while since it was lunch hour and their busy time of day, but she did eventually make it to their table. Anna told her about the closure of the events that started that night in her pub ten years ago. She was amazed at the story beginning with the death of Tommy Killern and ending with the death of Jack and Taryn. She thanked Anna for telling her about the story as she had promised she would.

After lunch they separated. Bridget and Fiona had things to do and Anna wanted to go back to the center. She felt that the longer she waited to go back to the scene of the crime, the harder it would be to do it. When she arrived at the house there were no other cars there. She used her new set of keys and entered through the front door and sat at the table where she had held her meeting just a short time ago. She had been there for mere minutes when the door opened and Shane came in. She stood and he rushed to her and wrapped his arms around her.

The hug lasted a longer time than might be appropriate for a man and someone else's wife. Anna pulled away, though if she were to be honest with herself, she didn't want to.

"I'm sorry. I had no right to do that. It's just that I've been so worried about you. When I found your car here and you were gone, I was afraid I'd never see you again."

"I understand that you found it and that you were the one who called the garda."

"I came because you dialed my number and hung up. If I'm to be completely honest, I was hoping the meeting was still going on and that I might get to talk to you after the others left. But the house was closed up and there was your car with the keys in it. I called Fiona's painter friend and then Fiona. She and Charles came here at once. Charles is the one who realized that your car had been tampered with. He fixed it, by the way. We called Garda Simms and told him what was happening and none of us slept all night. Look Anna, I know it's wrong of me to tell you this, but I have feelings for you. I know you're married so I will never act on my feelings, but while you were gone and we had no idea what was going to happen to you, I was beside myself."

"Shane don't. I'm in no condition right now to deal with this kind of information."

"I know. I'm sorry. I guess you need to get home to your husband. He's a lucky guy. He must have been worried sick."

Anna stepped away and picked up her purse to go. "I haven't seen or heard from him in days. He doesn't even know what happened. I have to go." She paused and turned back to him and asked, "Do you ride horses?"

"Of course I do. You're the second person who has asked me that in two days."

"Who else asked you?"

"Your friend Fiona."

She smiled and turned to go.

She went to the garda station and asked for Simms. When he arrived at the front of the station, he motioned to her to go back through to his office. "I hope you are feeling better today, Mrs. Kelly. You've had a difficult couple of days. I think if I were you I would be home lying down with a cold compress on my forehead and a drink in my hand. Is there something I can do for you?"

"It's my understanding that Jack and Taryn had no family left."

"That's right. We haven't been able to find anyone."

"Taryn told me as much. She said that she wanted me to take her child because she had no family and neither did Jack. The reason I ask is because I would like to take care of the funeral arrangements. If the law does allow me to adopt the baby, I don't want to have to take her to a pauper's grave to visit her birth parents. Can you tell me where the bodies were taken?"

"They haven't been released yet. I can see to it that they go to the funeral home of your choice."

She gave him the name of the home that had handled the deaths of members of her family in the past and he assured her that he would inform her when the bodies were transported. She felt a certain amount of urgency in the matter and so before she went home she visited the funeral home and found someone in the offices. There had been a viewing that afternoon and employees were available to make the necessary arrangements for when the time came.

"The circumstances are that the man committed two murders and the mother was aware of his crimes, so they were both criminals and they have no family other than a baby that was delivered just before the mother died. Therefore I have no need for an elaborate service. I just need to bury them with respect for the child they had. Some day she may want to go to their graves and she deserves to see that they were treated with dignity." She arranged for caskets and burial lots and asked that she be informed of the time of the burial. "We will just bury them without notice in the papers. I will, of course, attend. I want to be able to tell their daughter that I was there."

She was assured that as soon as the bodies arrived they would be prepared for burial and Anna would be notified so that plans could be made. As she was leaving the funeral home and walking toward her car she called her home and spoke to May. When she learned that her husband was not at home, she informed May that she would be getting something to eat on her own and that May was not to worry about her dinner. She went to the same fast food restaurant where she had first met Taryn and ordered a burger and a vanilla milkshake. She ate them in the car while thinking about the days since she had been there last.

She drove home and when she climbed the stairs, she went to the nursery that had been closed up like a time capsule. She looked at the things she had collected before she lost her baby, and decided that some of them were beautiful and timeless. Others would no longer suit her. She opened the curtains and pulled up the shades to let tomorrow's light into the room. She sat in the rocking chair thinking of how it will feel to hold the baby girl and rock her to sleep. As she rocked, the events of the day began to take their toll on her. After some time she got up and turned off the lights and walked across the hall to her bedroom. She changed into a camisole and a pair of boxer shorts and went straight to bed with a cold compress and a glass of wine. With thanks to Garda Simms she enjoyed them both and drifted off to much needed sleep.

28

Sunday morning was riding day with or without Carl. She wasn't going to allow his absence to ruin her Sunday plans. Anna had made arrangements the day before to have Fiona and Charles trailer her horse if necessary, since Carl had the Range Rover with him. Anna rose early and showered, did her hair and makeup and dressed in her riding clothes for the day. On her way to the stable to get her horse she called Fiona to see how soon she would arrive. As she made the turn in the driveway she stopped in her tracks. There, waiting for her with both horses already loaded, was Carl. He had a broad smile on his face and he greeted her with open arms.

"I guess I don't need transport after all," she said to Fiona. "Carl is here and ready to go to the ride. I'll see you there."

"Okay, Anna. Hang tough."

"I will."

Her husband rushed toward her and hugged her hard. "Anna, I have missed you so much," said Carl. "I have so much to tell you. It's all over. The problems we had to deal with are all behind us and I can tell you the whole story. Are you as happy to see me as I am to see you?" He was full of enthusiasm, perhaps too full to be sincere, but she was going to give him the benefit of the doubt up to a certain point.

"I guess I'll know that after I hear what has kept you from home and from calling. I really had no way of knowing if you were dead or alive. Some contact would have been nice. So what is the story?"

They both got into the Range Rover and Carl said, "I'll tell you all about it after the ride. There's too much story and not enough drive time. But believe me, it's all over. And what have you been up to since I saw you last?"

"I'll tell you later, too. Too much story and not enough drive time."

They arrived at Hal and Bunny Carson's home and drove back to the stables and parked in a spot suitable for unloading. The Carson's lived far enough out that almost everyone had had to transport their horses so the area was filled with trailers.

The Carson's had lived in total luxury on Walford Street in Dublin where the house they owned was a showplace for their extensive art collection. They lived in one of the most extravagant homes on the most extravagant street in town. Hal had built a computer software company from scratch, and when he and Bunny turned 55, they sold the company for more money than they ever imagined it would be worth. They wanted to simplify their lives, so they bought a property between Graent and Dublin with an old two story square cut stone home that was in need of TLC. They spared no expense in their renovations and the end result was a beautifully restored home that was one fourth the size of their previous home. They had furnished it with period pieces and of course their art collection. They had used a landscape artist to create grounds that required minimum maintenance.

The smaller home and the easy care yard made it possible to do it all themselves. Bunny learned to cook and Hal learned to mow his lawn. They had someone come in twice a week to clean, and twice a year they had a professional crew repair all of the mistakes Hal had made in the yard. But the real jewel of the property was the land that came with the house. They had three hundred acres of land that was part woods, part flat fields and part rolling hills crossed by a small running creek. Some country clubs hire people to design their golf courses. Bunny and

Hal hired someone to design a course so that a Sunday ride at their house involved trails carved out of the woods, paths through and across the stream in several places, and jumps with tracks going around them for those riders who wanted a leisurely ride and not a vigorous cross-country course.

Their stables were new. The ones that had been on the property were beyond repair, so they built a state of the art facility for horses with everything to make a horse comfortable, including air conditioning and a crystal chandelier. They did not build for over twenty horses, though, so Anna and Carl tied their horses to their trailer and tied a hay bag between them. They made their way to the garden behind the house with the other riders and helped themselves to breakfast. Carl acted as if nothing about their relationship had changed. He visited with friends and laughed at jokes. It made Anna furious, but she was determined to get through the day and hear what he had to say.

After the sumptuous meal was finished and everyone had had their fill of eggs, pastries, sausages, fruit, and much more, the riders went to the barn to ready their horses for the ride. When everyone had mounted up and toasted their hosts with champagne, Carl told Anna to go ahead with her friends. "I'm going to ride with Harvey Glavin. He's lagging a bit behind. He said that he had been a bit under the weather the last time we rode. I'll just ride along with him in case he has a problem. Besides, I know you and your friends want to chat." He leaned over and kissed her on the cheek before turning and going back to Harvey.

So the three women followed the pack and were soon out of sight of Carl. Bridget and Fiona wanted the whole story, but there wasn't one. "He hasn't told me yet. He said, 'There is too much story and too little drive time.' Can you imagine? I told him the same about what I had been doing and he didn't even ask about it. So he has no idea that I was held at gun point and knife point and held hostage and robbed. He apparently just believes that the world revolves around him and him only."

They rode for the day and after Anna's initial outburst, put the last week behind them. They talked about the baby and what Anna should name her, and they talked about the fact that Sarah was due home soon. Bridget and Fiona had parked their trailers on the north side of the barn and Anna and Carl were on the south side. So they said good bye at the end of the ride and made plans for Anna to contact them for lunch the next day so she could catch them up on all things Carl.

When Anna rode around the barn to where she thought the trailer was, she realized that it was gone. At that moment Harvey Glavin rode up alongside her and said, "Anna, my dear, Carl had to go home. He was feeling quite unwell. He didn't want to ruin your ride so he asked if I would take you and Gallant home. He made me promise not to tell you until the riding was over. He was so concerned that you have a good day." When he saw the reaction on her face, he misconstrued her meaning and said, "Don't worry Anna. I'm sure it was just something he ate. He will be fine. Let's get you home so you can see for yourself."

She readied and loaded her horse with Harvey's help and got into the passenger seat of his truck. They arrived at Kellenwood half an hour later and when her horse had been put in the barn for the night next to Carl's horse, she walked to the house and entered through the back door. There was no sign of life downstairs. She knew that May had left a sandwich for her as she always did after a ride, but she had no appetite for it. She climbed the stairs and went into the bedroom and stopped in her tracks. There on her pillow was an envelope with her name on it in Carl's handwriting. She wanted to run over to it and tear it open, but she knew somehow that as soon as she did her life was going to change drastically. She decided that whatever was in that envelope could only be faced after a long hot shower and a change of clothes. So after she finished, she dressed in a camisole and cotton pajama pants and with her hair hanging wet on her shoulders, she sat on the bed and hesitantly opened the letter and read.

29

My Dearest Anna,

 This is the most difficult thing I have ever had to do. I hope that when you finish reading this letter you will be able to forgive me for what I'm about to tell you. I want you to know that when all of this started, I had no intention of having it end this way.

 I told you this morning that at the end of the ride I would tell you the whole story. In fact, I believe that it will all be in the newspaper, if not tomorrow, then surely on Tuesday. So I won't go into it now. The attorney that I have been using will messenger papers to Charles in the morning that will outline what I have done for you. In the other attorney's defense I had him believing that I was doing what I was doing because I was dying and that I wanted to protect you after I was gone.

 I will say this much about my problems. They involve misuse of clients' funds. I am not proud of that, but it started out innocently and then mushroomed out of control. Eventually it got so big that there were only two options for me. One would be jail and the other would be to leave the country.

 My biggest concern in all of this is you. To that end I have done everything I can to protect you and the home you love. I believe I have taken legal steps that will insure that all of our property will be protected. The house, the cars, the money in the bank, even the horses, have been converted into single ownership in your name so that my crimes will not cause you to lose the things you love. I have also filled out forms allowing you to file for divorce with no contest. Contact Charles in *the morning and he will be able to tell you if I have done everything successfully. I wanted to use Charles since he is the best attorney I know, but I didn't want you to dislike or mistrust him for having done this for me without letting you know what was coming your way. I know you are going to need him in the near future.*

I left the ride early and came home today so that I could give myself time here with you out of the house to pack some things to take with me and to write this letter. You must understand that the hardest part of all of this is that I will be separated from you. But if I had been arrested and sent to prison I would still have been separated from you without my freedom. This way I will at least be free. I can't tell you where I'm going. If I did you would have to decide whether to tell the authorities or not. If you chose not to you would have to live with guilt. If you did tell them you might feel as if you had betrayed me. So I have taken that decision out of your hands.

You will not hear from me again. In this world of technology, any messages I might send to you could be tracked and without knowing it we could be giving away my location. So this is the last chance I will have to tell you how much I love you and how much our life together has meant to me. I will be free where I'm going, but my heart will always be a prisoner. Please try not to hate me, and some day in the future if you can find a way, please try to forgive me.

I wish you the very best. I hope you will find someone else to love, someone who will not betray you the way I have. I know you will have your friends around you and I am grateful for that. Charles will deal with all of the legalities and take care of you like a guard dog. It is only because I know how well protected you will be that I am able to leave you. I'm glad we had the chance to take that drive. I will be wearing the jacket you bought for me that day and it will always remind me of you.

Good bye my love, and live well.

Carl

When Anna finished reading her first thought was to call someone to come and help her through this horror. But instead she lay her head down on Carl's pillow and wept and eventually she fell asleep. When she awoke in the morning she saw the letter and wept again. But she was strong and she would survive this. She would have to for her new child. But Carl was right about one thing; she was going to need her friends and she was going to need Charles. So she got out of bed, took a shower, fixed her hair and makeup and dressed to the nines.

She went downstairs and May asked her what she wanted for breakfast. When May had fixed her scrambled eggs and a slice of toast, she put it in front of Anna where she sat at the counter. "May, I am going to tell you some things that might be hard to take. I suggest that you pour two cups of tea and sit down here with me."

May did as Anna had suggested and said, "What is it? Is something wrong?"

"Yes and no. Two things. Mr. Kelly is gone and will not be returning."

May sat stoically as if she already knew. "I had an idea when he didn't come home for days at a time, and then yesterday I saw him get into a taxi with several cases. I'm sorry Mrs. Kelly. I liked him very much."

"So did I, but as it turned out the person we liked so much didn't really exist. I can't go into detail about it. For one thing I have no details except that he has done something illegal and he has left the country. I would appreciate it if you would keep that to yourself for now, although it will probably be in the papers soon."

"Of course. You can count on me to keep your secret. What is the other thing?"

"The other thing is that there is going to be someone else moving in here. It will require you to do a thorough cleaning of the nursery." May certainly hadn't seen that one coming. "I am going to be adopting the daughter of a friend. The friend died just after delivering the baby and I was the one she chose to take care of her daughter. I had thought when I agreed that I would be raising her with my husband, but now I guess I'll be going it alone."

May put her hand over Anna's on the counter and said, "Not alone."

Anna started to get emotional at that and she had no time for emotions this morning. "I will tell you the details about that as well when I have a chance. Right now there are many things that I have to take care of regarding Mr. Kelly and the new baby, so I'm going to go into town and get started."

"I think having a baby in the house will be wonderful. I'm going to have to break out my knitting needles."

Anna smiled at that. Her parents were gone, but maybe she had built in grandparents for her child. She finished her eggs and toast and went to the study to make an appointment to see Charles. She told him about the letter briefly. She told him that Carl had left the country. He said he would see her whenever she got to his office. She told him she was on her way, and as she was leaving she saw May already taking her cleaning supplies up the stairs to get the nursery ready. As she left the house she found the newspaper still on the front steps. There didn't seem to be anything in it about Carl, so maybe she had a day's grace where he was concerned. There was an article that went into great detail about the murders that took place ten years ago, how they were solved, and that the killer had died in a fiery car crash after trying to rob a bank in town. Some details had been left out including the birth of the child and the mother's involvement. She was somewhat surprised to see that her name had been left out of the article as well. She wondered if she had Garda Simms to thank for that. Whoever was responsible had done her a favor. Surely it would come out at some point in the future. After all, she was known at the bank and the employees there could easily reveal her identity. But for now she had at least one day that she could come and go without worrying about dodging newspaper reporters.

30

Charles was waiting for her with a stack of papers on his desk. "Well, Anna, what a day this is. It's one I never thought I would see. I thought Carl was as honest as they came and I believed that the two of you would be together forever. He certainly pulled a fast one on all of us. What he has done is enough to put him in prison for many years. In a way I don't blame him for leaving the country."

Anna showed him the letter Carl had left for her. "Is he right? Did he protect me or am I going to lose my home? On one hand I don't want others to suffer for what Carl did to them, but I also don't want to suffer, especially now that I have a baby to think about. I need to know if I'm going to be able to keep my house."

"I have only had an hour to look over these papers, but from what I see he did what he said he did. I called the attorney who did this for him and made an appointment to see him this afternoon. I will know better then. But rest assured, I will take care of this. You will not have to pay for what he did. This does answer a question you asked me the other day, though."

"What was that?"

"You wanted to know why the guards at the bank seemed to be ready for you when you got there. My guess is that they were not actually waiting for you and your kidnappers. I think someone was on to what Carl was doing and they were hoping that he would come to take money out of the account, but when you showed up, they assumed you were getting money for Carl. They had a surprise when Jack showed them the knife."

"That makes sense. I know you will do whatever is right about all of this. But right now I need to know what has happened with the baby."

"Ah, I can give you good news on that front. I have papers here for you to sign, and others for you to show at the hospital so that you will be able to visit her and hold her. My friend in family court has taken care of everything and you will be fast tracked to adoption, and you will have legal permission to take care of her in the meantime. So the child will go home with you and not some strangers. Just present this at the hospital and everything should be taken care of. I will call you after I meet with Carl's attorney and give you an update. And please, join Fiona and me for dinner tonight. We'll invite Bridget and Daniel as well. Carl was certainly correct when he said that your friends would be there for you."

Anna's next stop was the hospital where she was allowed to hold her baby for the first time. She sat and rocked her for over an hour after she fell asleep. She then handed her over to a nurse and left the hospital in a much better frame of mind than when she had arrived. Her next stop was the house on Liffey.

Shane walked toward her slowly when she pulled up to the front of the house. He could tell something had changed. She started to tell him all about it, but the tears came and he pulled her to him and wrapped his strong arms around her. He just held her and that was the right thing to do. When she stopped crying he let her go and led her into the house. "This place looks wonderful," she said.

"I had a particular interest in doing this one right," he said.

"I'm going to tell you what has been going on in my life for the last couple of weeks. Some of it you know and some you don't, but I have to start at the beginning." She told him the entire story including the fact that her husband was on the run to avoid going to prison for illegal use of his clients' funds. Then she told him about what had happened to her while she was being held by Jack and Taryn. She told him about what happened at the bank and then the two accidents, the one that killed Taryn and the one that killed Jack. Then she told him that she was about to become a parent. He just listened. She liked that about him. Carl was always interrupting to ask questions or tell her she shouldn't have done what she did or try to fix things. But not Shane. When she was done his response was unexpected.

"I think you'll make a wonderful mother."

"That's it? That's all you have to say?"

"Like you said before, I already knew about Jack and Taryn, and I knew there was no way your husband could be away like he was if he planned to stay with you. There was something really fishy about that whole thing. The only part I didn't know was about the baby."

"Why didn't you say something about Carl?"

"It wasn't my place. Besides, you would have been angry if I had suggested that there was something going on with him. You would have said that I didn't know him, that I had only met him once, and you would have been right. I just know men. And I know that if I were married to you there is no way I would stay away like that and keep secrets from you. I would stick so close that you would get tired of seeing my face."

"Never."

"Never?" he asked walking toward her.

"Never." He kissed her then and she kissed him back.

"And babies love me."

They laughed and kissed again. And for the first time in days Anna felt as if things might turn out alright after all. The pressure that had started with the dead body in the backyard and ended with her husband fleeing the country seemed to fade away. She looked around her at the house that had started it all and leaned toward Shane for a deeper longer kiss.

EPILOGUE

It was a beautiful day for an open house. The sun was shining and the sky was full of white fluffy clouds. There was a crowd of around one hundred people standing in front of the Graent Arts Center on Liffey Street. The entire street was cordoned off and there was a party atmosphere. The backyard which had once been the temporary resting place of Tommy Killern was now filled with tables of finger foods and drinks ranging from water and soft drinks to champagne and Braunleaven wines donated in great quantity by her friend Sarah.

The gardens had been planted in colorful flowers and shrubs and the grass was like carpet. Her own gardener had taken great care in producing a landscape that was not only beautiful to look at, but would provide the photographers and painters in the center's classes with material for their artwork.

The banners and posters, as well as the brochures waiting inside had been done to perfection by her friend Bridget. They were colorful and represented the joy that Anna hoped would be brought to all of the people who participated in what the center had to offer.

Charles had handled all of her legal difficulties without her having to worry about a thing. Her friends had been her strength for the last months. They had been there night and day whenever Anna had needed a shoulder to cry on. And then there was Shane. He had said he would stick close and he had. And he had an uncanny ability to know just what she needed from him.

There was a ribbon strung across the gate to the front walkway and it was about to be cut. Anna approached it from the house side and asked for everyone's attention. She looked at the crowd of people in front of her. There were people she knew and people she didn't know. There were journalists and photographers there who were interested not in the problems Carl had caused for her and for everyone else affected by his crimes, but in the center and what it might mean to the town of Graent. There were people there who were interested in taking classes in pottery, stained glass, photography, painting, and whatever else might become part of the center. There were neighbors of the house who were happy to see it looking as glorious as it had when Anna's grandmother had been alive. There were people who were just curious or maybe interested in free food and drinks.

But most importantly, seated off to the side in a place of honor, were her friends Fiona, Bridget, and with a beautiful baby dressed all in pink on her lap, her very best friend Sarah. They were her support group. They were there for all the difficult times that Anna had faced in the months since Carl had left and they would be there for anything that might arise in the future. She didn't know what she would do without them.

And standing next to her was Shane, who after Anna said a few words about how happy she was that so many people had turned out to welcome the center to the community, would take the extra-large scissors along with Anna and cut the ribbon letting the crowd of people come forward and tour the center and meet the instructors who were waiting in their respective spaces.

As the crowd inched through the gates, many among them shaking her hand and offering congratulations and thanks for what she had done, she assessed her situation and thought that she had risen from the ashes better and happier than before. She thought about how now her life had purpose it hadn't had before. Not only did she have the Center up and running, but she had a beautiful baby who brought her such joy. She thought about how important her friends had been during her troubles and understood not for the first time how much she valued them. And she thought about Shane, whose strength had carried her through the difficult times. He had been welcomed by her friends and had even joined in the Sunday ride. It turned out that he does ride horses, and very well.

As she basked in her good fortune she turned and smiled at Shane. Her heart melted each time he looked into her eyes, and today was no exception. He took her hand in his, raised it to his lips, and looked toward the Center they had created together, and as if it represented the rest of their lives, he said, "Shall we?"

Made in the USA
Lexington, KY
08 March 2015